SLAYED

Also by Amanda Marrone

Uninvited

Revealers

Devoured

SLAYED

Amanda Marrone

Simon Pulse
NEW YORK LONDON TORONTO SYDNEY

SIMON PULSE

An imprint of Simon & Schuster Children's Publishing Division

1230 Avenue of the Americas, New York, NY 10020

First Simon Pulse paperback edition October 2010

Copyright © 2010 by Amanda Marrone

All rights reserved, including the right of reproduction in whole or in part in any form.

SIMON PULSE and colophon are registered trademarks of Simon & Schuster, Inc.

For information about special discounts for bulk purchases, please contact Simon & Schuster Special Sales at 1-866-506-1949 or business@simonandschuster.com.

The Simon & Schuster Speakers Bureau can bring authors to your live event. For more information or to book an event contact the Simon & Schuster Speakers Bureau at 1-866-248-3049 or visit our website at www.simonspeakers.com.

Designed by Mike Rosamilia

The text of this book was set in Cochin.

Manufactured in the United States of America

2 4 6 8 10 9 7 5 3 1

Library of Congress Control Number 2010928251

ISBN 978-1-4169-9487-9

ISBN 978-1-4169-9488-6 (eBook)

For Joe—you've been slaying me for years. Here's to many more!

Great big thanks to Jen Klonsky, Wendy Schmaltz, and everyone at Pulse for finding me. I'd never stake any of you—unless you were recruited by a vampire army and it was absolutely necessary—still not sure if I'd stake or behead you. Thanks to Nina and Pam for reading early on—you ladies rock. Much thanks to Joe for telling me about Ley Lines so the pieces could all fall together—couldn't have finished this without you.

1.

A storm-driven wave crashes up over the road and Dad swerves. Salt water hits the windshield of our ancient VW van, obliterating the view. My heart skips a beat as the van hydroplanes toward the rock-strewn edge bordering the ocean.

Mom gasps and her hand darts out to clutch Dad's arm. He turns the wipers on and the tires rumble as they make contact with the pavement again. He gives a nervous laugh. "That was a close one, eh?"

Mom drops her hand back to the folder in her lap. "Too close. I'd like to get to South Bristol in one piece."

Dad briefly turns his head toward me in the back. "Hope I didn't scare you, Doodlebug. We should be turning off the coast road in about five miles and the station isn't much past that."

"Mm," I grunt, not bothering to ask him to drop the "doodlebug" thing for the millionth time. But seriously, how hard is it to say "Daphne"?

He nods and I watch him push his glasses up the bridge of his nose in the rearview mirror. My eyes briefly linger on the ragged scar on his neck before I turn away, glad he's not going to try and engage me in meaningless banter. My stomach is wound too tight anticipating the horrors of our next job. I lean forward and rifle through my duffel bag for the container of multicolored antacids. I force myself to swallow the chalky bits and wait for my stomach to settle.

Mom pushes her reddish-brown hair behind her ears. She opens the folder and continues skimming through the papers the police faxed us last night at the hotel in Buffalo. "Huh," she says absentmindedly. "Strange. Very strange." She makes ticking noises with her tongue on the roof of her mouth. "I wish I'd had more time to go through this before we said we'd come. From what I'm reading, I think we should have given them a higher quote."

Bureaucracy being what it is, the dossier is a bazillion pages longer than it needs to be. All they really need to write is *"Come quickly. Here's who to call for body-bag pickup...."* Instead, they send page after page of insurance clauses, twisted lawyer-lingo and other indecipherable nonsense before they even get to the part detailing the actual problem—*vampires*.

It's *always* vampires, and useless details about the town's liability clauses won't change how we stake them.

I wait for Mom to say more but she just turns to the next page. I have to admit I'm a bit curious; this is the first time she's used the word "strange" on what I assumed was a standard stake-'em-and-bag-'em job.

I'm tempted to ask her what's up, but instead look out at the ocean. The last thing I want to do is give the impression I'm actually interested in this or any of our jobs. Steel gray waves capped with frost-white foam churn and thunder against the shore, violent in the wake of a late spring nor'easter that's made its way up the coast. I hope it isn't a sign that things will go down badly like the Oak Hill gig.

I shake my head. Oak Hill was a major game-changer for me.

Nothing like hicks getting suckered by vampires—literally and figuratively—to give a kid a major reality check.

Squeezing my eyes shut tight, I try to banish the images that are seared into my brain as if it all just happened. Five years ago we blew into Oak Hill on the tail of a tornado—eerie yellow sky—gale-force winds throwing debris in the path of our van. That town—population twenty-eight—is where my twelve-year-old self finally realized my parents weren't invincible and that when dealing with vampires, you can go from hunter to hunted in a blink of an eye.

You could say Oak Hill was the end of my childhood—twisted as it was. But when I saw a vampire actually rip a flap of skin from my father's neck, saw the blood pour from the wound and stain his white shirt, I finally realized any hunt could be our last.

Dad coughs and I turn and look at his reflection in the rearview mirror again. He lifts his chin slightly to look up at the stoplight and I follow the edges of the white scar on his neck with my eyes. Whenever Dad complains about the sloppy stitch-job Mom did, she jokes that he should have married a plastic surgeon.

They both think this is inexplicably hilarious—somehow forgetting that we could have lost him that day if I hadn't been able to cut the head off the vampire trying to feed on him.

But I guess being a descendent of Dr. Abraham Van Helsing—aka vampire slayer extraordinaire—you have to laugh or go crazy. Since Dad is a direct descendent of Dr. Van Helsing it makes some sense that he'd keep up the family business—it's all he knew growing up. I'm not sure what Mom's deal is. She refuses to talk about her past or her family. I figure something pretty bad must've gone down for her to have actually chosen this life.

Traveling the country slaying vamps might sound exciting in a video game sort of way, but after cutting off the heads of endless vamps it gets old. And knowing each job might be your last, well, either you can take it in stride or you can spend that traveling time imagining a different life.

I look down on the floor of the van at a crate filled with my meager belongings, and pull out the worn purple binder. I open it and sigh. I've landed on a picture I drew when I was seven—a yellow house with a white dog sitting in the yard. I used to imagine going into some town and finding that house. My parents would see it and, without knowing why, fall in love with it, and decide it was finally time to settle down and give me a normal upbringing. I imagined siblings with whom I'd argue over the TV remote or whose turn it was to walk that white dog. My best friend and I would sometimes fight over boys, but we'd always make up.

I turn the pages and look at the various drawings of "best friends" I'd made over the years—always side-by-side with a crayon or color-penciled "me"—my long, red hair loose and wavy around my shoulders instead of pulled back in its usual practical braid. It's beyond pathetic, but

I still know each girl's name and the imagined adventures we shared.

None of which involved anything with sharp teeth or blood.

I stare at the picture I drew of a girl with brown skin and tight, dark curls forming a halo around her face — Kayla. How many times had I looked for her in real life? I wanted her — or any of them — to be real so badly I ached, and I wished on countless stars hoping to bring them to life. And in every town we were in, I searched the streets hoping to see one of them in the flesh so I'd know I'd finally found *home*.

See? Crazy.

I flip through some more pages until I get to the more current pictures. Real girls — well as real as models can be — torn from the pages of *Jennifer-Kate* magazine. It's the only magazine Mom will let me read because she says it isn't all sexed-up like the other ones lining the supermarket racks.

I'm not sure what she's so worried about. Unless you count vampires, policemen, and an assortment of fast-food cashiers, hotel clerks, and creepy gas-station attendants, my experience with boys is pure fantasy, and really I would give *anything* to read those sexed-up magazines to find out what actual girls are doing with actual boys.

But former high-fashion model Jennifer-Kate pledges on the cover of each issue to "Keep it clean!" I saw her biography on TV last year. She started modeling at fourteen, hit rehab at sixteen, and started the magazine in her forties to give girls a taste of fashion without exposing them to the "Hollywood fast lane to hell."

I happen to think Jennifer-Kate is a sanctimonious killjoy, and if I ever meet her I will laugh in her perfectly botoxed face, because articles singing the praises of "The ten best things about holding hands" or "What your favorite lip gloss says about you!" is beyond sad. Jennifer-Kate at least got to experience life — bumps and all. But I'm seventeen and utterly *desperate* for any lascivious information about the opposite sex I can get my hands on, and all I can get is her pathetic G-rated articles.

At least the clothes in the magazine are cool, but thank goodness for late-night cable TV in hotel rooms or I would be totally clueless about guys. Not that I believe everything I see, but some of it has to be true, right?

As I turn the pages in the binder, I trace my fingers over every impractical hairstyle and hot outfit I'll never get to wear because my wardrobe is a sad combination of Wal-Mart rollbacks and thrift-store dregs. And as much as I covet designer shoes, high heels and hunting definitely don't mix.

I take out a small pair of scissors and the latest issue of *Jennifer-Kate* from the crate to add some new pictures to my binder.

According to the cover, *"Prom season is coming"* and I can have *"a good time without going all the way."*

Of course I have watched enough prom movies to know that this is total crap—even with psychotic serial killers on the loose, prom is all about hooking up.

I turn to the page I've folded over in the dress section and spread the magazine open on my lap. I'm filled with longing for things I'll never have, but I tell myself to keep dreaming.

"You will go to prom," I whisper.

The first dress in the two-page spread is a light purple, one-shouldered, Greek goddess–style gown with a gold belt to cinch the waist. The moment I saw it I knew it was the perfect one for me. I open the scissors, slide one blade carefully along the crease to cut the page out, and then insert it in the opening of the plastic sleeve in the binder.

I turn to page eighty-one for the hairstyle—long, spiral curls. I don't have a curling iron or hot rollers (Mom says we can't afford to spend money on anything so frivolous) but if I want my hair to look like the model's I can't afford *not* to have one.

After I add the hairstyle to the binder I turn back to

page six to admire my "date," a totally drool-worthy guy with a strong chiseled chin and straight blond hair framing ice-blue eyes that look into my soul. I stare at his six-pack abs above the pair of low-slung jeans he's modeling.

I study his face and decide he looks like a "Brad."

In my head I've dressed (and undressed) *Brad* in the dark gray tux on page one hundred twenty countless times this week. But Brad and I have no intention of going to the parent-sponsored after-prom party Jennifer-Kate insists is a *"totally fun and safe way to party."*

Instead, I giggle as he kisses my neck in the elevator on the way up to the fancy hotel room he booked for us. I burn with anticipation as he opens the door revealing a petal-strewn bed. He slides the dress off my shoulder and the satin caresses my skin as it falls to the floor. I step out of the fabric piled gracefully around my feet and he kisses me hungrily as we fall onto the bed with my six-inch heels still on. The scent of roses fills the air as our bodies press together. His lips devour every inch of my nearly naked—

"Make a slight right onto route 1B and continue for one mile," the GPS announces.

"We should be there shortly, Doodlebug," Dad says. "Make sure you have everything you need."

I throw my magazine back into the crate as my cheeks burn. "Yeah, okay," I choke out.

I quickly put everything else back, secure the knife strapped to my calf, and make sure it's fully covered.

Reality check.

There will be no corsages, limos, fancy dresses, extreme heels, or impossibly hot Brads in my future. Only fangs, decapitated heads, traveling the country with my parents in this shit-can van packed with boxes of garlic, and sleeping in connecting hotel rooms—alone.

Sucks to be me.

Mom's cell phone rings and we all sit up straight. We don't get a lot of calls. "It's the Bristol Police," she says, a hint of concern in her voice. She takes a deep breath and then opens her phone. "Joy Van Helsing—may I help you?"

She nods. "As a matter of fact we're almost there." She pauses and turns to my father, wide-eyed. "We had a verbal agreement," she huffs into the phone. "And we've come all the way from *Buffalo*."

Dad looks briefly at her, shaking his head. "I knew we should have had them wire the money first," he says a little too loudly. "There was something fishy about this one."

Mom waves her hand to quiet him and I lean forward so I don't miss anything. I'm hopeful this job might be canceled.

"Well, that's ridiculous. You got our résumé and referrals—we're government licensed and have a reputation for being discreet. No one in town will be any the wiser as to why we're there."

I try to hear the muffled voice coming from her phone but can't make anything out.

"That *incident*," Mom snaps, "happened *thirteen* years ago when there was another person working with us, but I can assure you our record has been spotless since."

She scoffs. "And how many vampires have *you* slayed?"

I can't make out the muffled reply but I'm pretty sure he's said—none. Most cops don't even want to attempt to mess with vampires.

"Anyway," Mom continues, "I'd love to know where you're getting this *information* from." She listens for a few seconds, her eyes narrowed. "Well, Officer MacCready, I happen to know a few things about *Mr. Harker* that he's most likely left off his resume that might affect your decision about who is the best candidate to handle this job. If you'll just give us a bit of your time we'd be happy to speak to you about it."

A small smile breaks out on Mom's face—something I see so rarely. "Wonderful. We'll see you in a few minutes." She shuts her phone and tosses it roughly in her purse, all business now. "Nathan Harker—after all these years! What the *hell* is he thinking moving in on our territory and bad-mouthing us to the police?"

"I can't believe he'd do something like that," Dad says quietly. "Not after everything we've been through."

"Like Nathan cares about our past!" Mom shoots back. "And I haven't a doubt in my mind he's burned every bridge of his out west so he had no choice left but to move on to our territory without a moment's care about how it would affect us."

"Joy," Dad says, his voice full of warning. "Let's—"

Mom scoffs. "What? Let's forget what happened? Not possible!"

"Who are you talking about, Mom?" I ask.

She turns to me and I see her pupils are wide and dark. "*The Harkers*. Nathan and Tyler Harker."

"*Harker?*" I ask. "As in *Jonathan* Harker, one of the slayers of Dracula?"

Mom takes a deep breath. "Unfortunately, yes. Although I'd bet good money Jonathan Harker is turning in his grave knowing his great-grandson screwed up so badly he had to stake his own wife!"

"Joy, please!" Dad admonishes. "This isn't the time or the place. . . ." His worried eyes connect with mine in the rearview mirror.

"She's old enough, Vince, and if Nathan is going to be moving in on our territory, she needs to know what kind of a man he is. I can only imagine what's become of the boy."

Dad shakes his head. "Look, we're almost at the station, let's find out what's going on and then you and I can discuss the best way to handle the Harker situation."

Mom looks out the window, chewing on a hangnail. "Fine. Hopefully he's still got a ways to go before he arrives in town."

I lean all the way forward and look between the two of them. "Wait a minute. You guys can't leave me hanging like this! What did the Harkers do? And what happened thirteen years ago?"

"Let's just say we used to work with the Harkers but parted company after our divergent methods of hunting became too big to overcome."

"But what about his wife?" I continue. "Is it really true he had to . . . stake her?"

Dad sighs.

"Yes, he did," Mom says.

I lean back in my seat and stare at my parents. I'd imagined losing them hundreds of times to a vampire attack, but it never once occurred to me that they would get turned and one of us would have to . . .

I shudder. It makes sense. We often split up to get a job done faster or scout out an area. It would be easy to get turned and catch someone by surprise and what else could you do but . . .

A small laugh escapes my mouth. "Well, let's just hope Dad never has to go there."

"Daphne!" Dad says.

"Sorry," I say bitterly. "But it's not like it isn't a possibility." Anger wells up inside me like a crashing wave. For the millionth time I wonder why they didn't quit after I was born and get some freaking normal jobs. Any jobs. Hell, I'd live in the worst trailer park in the world and proudly say my parents flip burgers for a living instead of doing this.

"Could you stake me?" I ask, the words coming out before I can stop them.

Dad shoots a look at Mom. "You had to go there."

"This is Harker's fault, not mine," she insists.

"Could you?"

Mom turns around and faces me. Her cheeks are flushed and her jaw is clenched. "Yes, Daphne, I could."

I look away from her, shaking my head. "I wish I could say I'm surprised," I whisper.

Dad pulls the van into the police station parking lot and cuts the engine. He puts both of his hands on the top of the steering wheel and then rests his forehead on them.

We sit in silence for a few minutes and then Mom unbuckles her seat belt. "Daphne, you know what we're up against. You know why we do this," she says as she organizes the paperwork in her lap.

I look down at the binder filled with dreams and hopes I'll never get to live. "I know why it has to be done; I just don't know why it has to be *us*."

Mom looks up at the roof and Dad reaches out and takes her hand. She bows her head and leans into him. "Who better than us?"

"It's not fair," I say. "Why don't I get to choose whether or not I want to do this?"

"Look, Daphne, your mom and I each have our reasons. There have been some things from our past we wanted to *shield* you from—maybe that was the wrong approach. Maybe you'd be more accepting of what we do if we'd been up front with you."

"Enough coddling her," Mom says. "Daphne, we *need* this job. You know how tight money is. And with what the Harkers have told the police, we're going to have some explaining to do. I just hope you're mature enough to hear what we have to say and conduct yourself properly during the interview. None of your sulking. It was embarrassing watching your eye-rolling in the Buffalo office; that's not the kind of behavior that will persuade someone to give us work. "

"Fine!" I snap.

"Maybe she should wait in the car," Dad says. "We can talk to her later."

Mom scoffs. "They're expecting three slayers for the briefing. She's coming with us." She pulls down the sun visor and tilts her chin up, applying fresh lipstick in the faded mirror. She purses her lips and then flips the visor back up. "Are we ready?"

"Does my hair look okay?" I ask sarcastically. "Wouldn't want to make a bad impression."

Mom gives Dad an *ignore her* look and then they get out of the car. I shake my head, almost wishing I'd inherited Mom's robotic lack of emotion. I open the door and think about the job we're trying to secure, and all the jobs we've been on. My stomach churns and I swallow back some bile rising in my throat. What fresh nightmares could my parents have tried to *shield* me from? What could possibly be worse than this?

2.

"So you see," Mom continues, "it wasn't negligence on our part; we simply didn't realize how far gone my father-in-law was."

Officer MacCready sips his coffee and then swishes it around noisily in his mouth. "Leaving someone in his condition alone for any amount of time is never a good idea, and given his background, leaving him with a child—why, I might go so far as to call it gross negligence."

Mom shakes her head rapidly. "No. I freely admit that was a *misjudgment* on our part. But you have to understand the pressure cooker we were in. And he'd never left a hotel room before so we had no reason to believe he'd leave."

Officer MacCready picks up a sheet of paper on his

desk. "But he did, and that little *misjudgment* caused an innocent person to get staked. I know you people are working under extreme conditions, but that is a serious safety issue. You get full government healthcare; it would've been easy to have him committed."

Dad nods but doesn't say anything, and I can't believe what I'm hearing. I guess this is why Dad hardly ever talks about his father. Vince Van Helsing Sr.—his brain destroyed by dementia—left me alone in a hotel room and staked a fourteen-year-old honor student, thinking she was a vampire.

Un-freaking-believable.

I stare straight ahead and try to reconcile the vague memories I have of my grandfather reading to me in hotel rooms with the fact that he murdered an innocent person. I was four when he was taken away by the police. Mom told me he was going to a nursing home. I guess I should be thankful they spared me the gory details of what really happened.

Mom sits up and folds her arms across her chest. "No question it was a horrific incident, but the bottom line is my husband and I were not directly involved and we were cleared of any wrongdoing. As you can see from our résumé our record has been spotless and citizens' comp payouts have been minimal. The fact that Nathan Harker brought this to your attention yet failed to mention his own unorthodox approach to extermination which resulted in having to stake his wife as she was attacking their own son speaks for itself."

My mouth drops open and a queasy feeling overtakes me. This is getting worse by the second. I knew Mom would bring this up to help secure the job, but hearing her laying it out there—that Mrs. Harker was killed as she was actually trying to . . .

I bite my lip and try to erase the image from my head.

"Well," Officer MacCready says calmly, like this isn't stomach-turning news, "I called the folks heading up the Midwest/West Coast Vampire Control and that Harker fellow has himself a *bit* of a reputation. Seems he had a drinking problem. Authorities threatened to take his son, but . . ." He appraises Mom and Dad. "Well, you know how the government cuts you *specialists* some slack in the child-rearing department, among other things."

Dad clears his throat. "Daphne here passed her GEDs with a ninety-five percent, and got her diploma at age fifteen. We in no way slacked off on her education."

Officer MacCready's eyes drift over to where I'm sitting in a corner and I turn away. It's obvious he has little respect for my parents—can't say as I blame him. Few people stick with the vampire-slaying gig for long, but those who do are given tremendous leeway about how they run their affairs, including looking the other way while bringing children on hunts.

"Harker is a bit of a loose cannon," Officer MacCready continues. "He's been written up for quite a few unnecessary stakings made in front of citizens and you know the municipalities hate having to pay the comp money to keep people from talking, but he also has the ability to clean a town up quickly." He shakes his head. "It kills me when the federal government refuses to foot the bill. Like we have crystal balls that can predict vampire infestations when we do our yearly budgets? Add in a bad winter where any surplus we had goes to snow removal and we're screwed." He leans back and his computer chair groans under his considerable weight. "Where the hell are we supposed to come up with comp money?"

"Well," Dad says, "there *are* times when dispatching vampires in front of citizens is unavoidable."

Officer MacCready nods. He pats his large belly with his hands as he looks back and forth between my parents. "I suppose you're right, but if I can't get an assurance that the folks here in town aren't going to be exposed to a staking and beheading, what's to keep me from hiring Harker? His bid came in a thousand dollars under yours.

He had a lot of ideas about all of those babies ending up in the hospital too."

I lean in, wondering if this was the "strange" stuff Mom was muttering about.

"Sounded like Harker knew what he was talking about," Officer MacCready continues.

Mom takes a sharp intake of breath and exchanges a quick look with Dad. "We'll match his price."

"What?" I gasp.

Officer MacCready smiles. Even though we do get perks like full medical coverage, our fees are determined by how much a town can afford. With the recession showing little improvement and slayers underbidding each other, money has been tight. Mom and Dad keep talking about some of the repairs the van needs so I know knocking that much money off our fee is killing her. This also means I won't be getting a cut like they promised, which means no curling iron and maybe even no magazines.

Mom and Dad have a great reputation, so even though there are at least a dozen other licensed slayers getting calls for bids, we usually get the higher paying gigs. Apparently the Harkers have something of a reputation too.

Mom folds her hands in her lap and puts on her best I-know-what-I'm-talking-about face. "And I've been giving the other problem a lot of thought. If your local children are falling prey to a mysterious malaise, I'm thinking there may be psychic vampires feeding off their energy much like a parasite."

Officer MacCready sucks some coffee through the gap in his front teeth. "According to Harker, attacks on children like this by energy or pyschic vampires are almost unheard of, yet we've had sixteen infants hospitalized for anemia and unexplained weakness— four more this week—and no common denominator connecting the victims. With the influx of vampires our little town has attracted recently, Harker thinks something else is involved."

"Well, it could be a number of things," Mom says. She starts fussing with the papers in the folder, obviously trying to buy some time to think.

I'd heard Mom and Dad talk about psychic vampires before and I think Mr. Harker is right. Most psychic "vampires" aren't vampires at all, just everyday people who for one reason or another have never been able to maintain their physical or mental energy and wind up "sucking" energy from their friends, family, or coworkers.

Dad said a lot of times these people are controlling or emotionally needy, but some aren't even aware they're doing it. I don't know a lot about it, but besides being all kinds of wrong, sucking energy from an infant doesn't sound very satisfying and I can't help but wonder what the Harkers think is going on.

Dad clears his throat. "Did Mr. Harker share his thoughts with you?"

Officer MacCready shakes his head. "He didn't go into detail but you can ask him yourself."

He beckons with his hand and I turn to follow his gaze. A man is peering at us through the window next to the door. He nods and a cocky smile breaks out on his face. He struts in and I take an immediate dislike to him. He's wearing a long, black trench coat over a dark turtleneck, jeans, and heavy black boots. His thinning hair is greased back and he looks—and smells—like he's in need of a good night's sleep and some body wash. His skin is paler than mine and his sunken eyes are underlined with dark circles.

"Vince, old buddy, it has been too long," he says, "and Joy, looking good as ever."

Mom jumps up and looks mad enough to charge, but Dad puts a hand on her arm and she simply stares the man down. "*What* are you doing here, Nathan?" she asks.

He smiles and fidgets with what I'm assuming is his wedding ring. "Same as you, looking for work. Seems we'd been doing such a good job out west that all the gigs dried up. I tried some construction work but that just ain't for me, so the boy and I decided to expand our territory."

"Seems to me," Mom spits, "you got a reputation for being a jackass and couldn't find any 'gigs' so you had to crash ours. We had an agreement to stay in our own territories."

Nathan Harker bows his head. "That was a long time ago, Joy, and I have to go where the work is. Surely you can't fault me for that."

Before Mom can answer, his eyes find mine. My cheeks redden as he looks me up and down and a slimy smirk breaks out on his face. "Are you your mother's daughter or what?" He laughs and slaps his knee. "Spitting image." He turns to Mom. "Bet she's got your fiery temper to go with that red hair."

Suddenly the room erupts in yelling. Mom is in Mr. Harker's face and Dad is trying to pull her back, begging her to calm down. Officer MacCready whistles loudly and everyone turns to him. "Folks, if you all were hoping to impress me, you're going about it the wrong way. Let's have a seat and discuss this like mature adults."

Mom's chest heaves up and down while Mr. Harker nods and smiles. "I would like nothing more than that," he says. "I'm sure we can work out an amicable agreement."

Mom wipes her mouth like she's trying to rid herself of a bad taste and stalks over to me. "Daphne, I don't see any reason why you can't start on reconnaissance. You know the drill."

"But we don't have the job yet," I say quietly. I look over her shoulder and see everyone is watching us.

"We will," she says. "And the sooner we can get this over with the better. Go."

I nod and grab my large purse off the chair. "Okay. I saw a pub when we pulled into town. I'll start there."

I shut the door on my way out and let out a long sigh. What a freaking mess!

"Hey," a voice says right behind me.

I jump and turn around, heart pounding. A greasy-haired boy about my age smiles down at me hesitantly. He's wearing a long, stained trench coat identical to Mr. Harker's so I'm guessing this is his son. I try to remember what Mom said his name was, but decide it doesn't matter. He's got jerk written all over him just like his father.

I look him up and down the way his father did to me and take in the tragic Goth look he's sporting. Head to toe black complete with tight jeans and T-shirt emphasizing his skinny frame, *guy-liner*, keys hanging from a chain off his belt loop, and a skull-and-crossbone–adorned messenger bag for which I decide to cut him some slack because he does need to carry his stakes and knives in something. "You always sneak up behind people?"

He smiles wider. "Ha, yeah, that wasn't real smart of me." He leans in close. "Lucky for me you didn't pull a stake out," he whispers like this is supposed to be funny.

I take a step back—the guy definitely needs a shower. "I gotta go."

I turn and he puts a hand on my arm. "Wait."

"Get off me!" I say, yanking my arm away from him.

He holds his hands out in front of him as if he's going to deflect a punch. "Hey, I'm sorry. I shouldn't have done that, but I just wanted to talk." He runs his fingers through his hair, pushing his long bangs aside. "It didn't sound like things were going too well in there. My dad was hoping we could all, you know, work together."

I give him an incredulous look. "Are you for real? Your dad tried to sabotage this job for us and he thought we'd want to team up and go all Hardy Boys/Nancy Drew mystery special together?"

He bites his lip and looks down at the floor. "He kind of panicked when he heard it was your family that was going to be here. And he only said that stuff because we really need the work. He was kicking himself for it afterward, really, but he was also hoping maybe . . ." He shrugs.

"You know what I hope?"

He peers out at me from behind his bangs.

"I hope you two go back where you came from and leave us the hell alone. Now if you'll excuse me, I have some recon to do."

I storm down the hall and push the outside doors open as hard as I can. The cool air smells of low tide and my head starts to clear. That guy is seriously deluded. I can't believe he even had the nerve to try to talk to me after what his father did.

What an idiot.

I walk through the parking lot to the main street and admire the red-tinged clouds hanging in the darkening sky. I check the sunset schedule Mom printed out—the sun officially set fifteen minutes ago. It would be nice to go to the nearby dock and look out over the water and watch the stars come out, but I've got work to do. I undo my braid and put my hair band in my coat pocket. I shake my hair out and then reach into my purse for some red lipstick. I swipe it on and take a quick peek in my hand mirror. Amazing what some lipstick does to make me look a little older.

I zip up my purse and head for the pub. Hanging out in the local drinking holes is a great way to overhear gossip and look for vamps trolling for dinner. I'd already loaded my wallet with my fake Maine driver's license and several credit cards to give the illusion that not only am I old enough to drink, but I'm also poised to ruin my credit by maxing out all my cards like so many other twenty-one-year-olds I'll be pretending to be.

As I approach The Rusty Rudder, I pass an alley and catch a glimpse of a bright pink car. In some parts of the country pink cars aren't that unusual, but the color seems glaringly out of place in northern Maine. Curiosity gets the better of me, and I turn back and duck into the alley dividing the pub and a bookstore. I unzip my purse and put one hand on a stake because finding vamps skulking in dark alleys is fairly common in *any* part of the country. Drunk guys pissing behind bars and restaurants make for perfect victims. It's sad the number of drained bodies we've found with their pants around their knees.

As I get closer I see it's a Cadillac—with a purple THE DISCO UNICORNS magnetic sign on the bumper—parked next to a Dumpster stinking of rotting food and stale beer.

The Disco Unicorns are a kiddie-rock band that I absolutely loved when I was little. They had their own TV show. It was hard not to wish I was one of the kids singing and dancing in the Unicorns' Pink Pony Playhouse instead of watching my parents sharpen stakes or wipe blood off knives in whatever cheesy motel we happened to be staying at.

The driver is in the front seat blowing smoke out his window. He looks like a pretty big, burly guy and I wonder why on earth he's driving a pink caddie with a Disco Unicorn emblem for all to see. As I head back to the pub a smile comes to my lips, and I hum the tune to their "Pineapple Pizza Picnic" song; one of my favorites—and one Dad used to sing to me.

I remember the day he took Mom and me to a restaurant and ordered pineapple pizza, something I thought only existed in the Disco Unicorn world—and something Mom came down on him for because the pineapple cost a whopping two dollars extra.

When I get to the sidewalk I look to see if that Harker kid is lurking around in his stupid trench coat stalking me. I spot him leaning on the rails by the end of the dock peering out at the sky—apparently not looking for me at all.

As I pull open the door to the pub, overly loud music and voices spill out and I remember his name.

Tyler.

3.

Inside The Rusty Rudder, a loud group is playing pool and laughing. A few people sit alone or in pairs, and a girl with white-blond hair is arguing loudly with the bartender. I've seen this scene played out at countless bars before and know it's only a matter of time before Blondie will be forcibly bounced out for being intoxicated—which she will vehemently and loudly deny.

It's never pretty.

I decide to ask for a seat near the pool table. The waitress comes over and I get ready for the drill.

"I'm Shelly and I'll be your server tonight. Can I get you something?" she asks.

"I'll have whatever the Sam Adams seasonal is—on tap if you have it."

"Do you have a driver's license?" she says without missing a beat. She stares me down like she knows I'm underage and completely wasting her time.

I nod and take out my fake ID. "Here ya go."

Shelly gives my license a quick once-over and hands it back.

"I'll be back in a minute," she says.

My parents have instructed me to order alcohol to "blend in," but have made me promise to drink very little because I'm only seventeen. I've been on "bar" duty for a year, and it's such a relief to be away from my parents and pretend I'm a grown-up for a while. I turn my attention to the crowd at the pool table. They're overly loud, but unfortunately, it's mostly giggling by the girls and posturing by the guys—nothing about vampires, missing persons, or the kids in the hospital.

Everyone else seems to be consuming their drinks—so no vamps in here at the moment. Vamps will order a drink and bring the glass to their lips but take only very tiny sips.

They prefer blood.

The pool table crowd suddenly stops talking. One brunette with her hair in a ponytail gently elbows her friend and they both look toward the bar. The bleach blonde who was arguing with the bartender is weaving her way toward them and they stifle a laugh.

"Oh, God, here she comes," the brunette says.

"Booty call, Gabe," another girl says.

Two guys fist bump while another in ripped jeans and a flannel shirt holds a pool cue up to his mouth like a microphone and starts singing an off-key rendition of "Jelly-Bean Jamboree" which was another one of my favorite Disco Unicorn songs. I look around trying to figure out the connection to The Disco Unicorns but come up empty.

"You suck, Gabe," Blondie says, but she's smiling at him.

The guy in flannel puts the pool cue to his lips and licks the handle. "Actually, I was hoping *you'd* suck," he answers back with a wink.

He leans in and tries to kiss her but she pushes him away and then jumps up to sit on the edge of the pool table. I cringe and hope she's wearing underwear because her skirt is way too short. "Asshole," she says, but it's obvious she's enjoying it all.

My mind scrambles. I could swear I've seen her before, but I think I'd remember boobs that big. She leans back and sticks out her chest. "I'm bored," she says.

"Why don't you get a job?" the brunette asks.

The other girl eyes Blondie. "From the looks of her outfit I'd say she's working—how much are you gonna pay her tonight, Gabe?"

My mouth drops open as the two girls laugh.

Blondie sits up, sways a bit and then flips them off with both hands. "Fuck off, bitches. Hope your moms are having fun cleaning rooms at the Motel 6; they're due to scrub all seven toilets at my house tomorrow."

The girls stop laughing and one of them flips her back, but they get quiet and move toward the bar followed by two of the guys.

"Gabe, *darling*, you've got to stop slumming it with those harpies," she says. She pulls him over to her and wraps her legs around him and starts singing an X-rated version of "Jelly-Bean Jamboree."

I can hardly believe this. I'm here to see if there's any scoop on the local vamps; instead I'm listening to some trashy girl singing about jelly beans and *sex*—which is totally messing with my G-rated memories of the song. Shelly brings me my beer and I take a big swig—sorry, Mom and Dad.

Shelly tilts her head toward the girl. "Try to ignore her. She does this almost every night, but from the looks of it she'll be leaving pretty soon with her *friend*. You know how it is—famous parents, ridiculously spoiled, party animal kid. It's sad, really; she was so nice when she was little."

I stare at the girl for a few seconds and then my mouth drops open. "Oh, my God. Is that *Maybelle Crusher*?" I whisper. Maybelle was the daughter of the lead singers of The Disco Unicorns. She used to sing with her parents on the TV show, but when season three started she was inexplicably replaced by a perky blonde named Sugar LeBlanc who I never warmed up to because her smile was always too big and forced-looking.

"That's Maybelle all right," Shelly says.

My heart skips a beat. I found one of my "friends."

There's a picture of Maybelle and me dancing in the Pink Pony Playhouse in my binder. I look over at Maybelle grinding herself against Gabe on the pool table and feel like the wind just got knocked out of me. All the years I dreamed of finding one of my "friends" in real life and when I finally do, she's a foul-mouthed—hate to say it—ho. Of course, given my long history of broken dreams, I'm not sure why this should surprise me.

Life is so not fair.

Shelly cracks her gum. "She goes by Kiki now. Got her name officially changed and everything. A lot of people don't make the connection; too much plastic surgery and bleach." She points to my beer. "I'll take slinging drinks over the life that kid must have had any day. All the money and opportunity in the world and she's *here*, making an ass of herself."

Shelly saunters away and I glance at *Kiki* making out with Gabe. I quickly turn away and gulp some more of my beer. I take another peek and shake my head. I'm figuring she can't be more than five feet tall. I think she had the bump removed from the bridge of her nose and she's gone overboard with the bleach. On the show, she had this super shiny brown hair, but now Kiki Crusher looks like a hoochie Barbie doll.

Kiki comes up for air and pushes Gabe away. "Hey!" she calls out as Shelly passes her. "Can you get me another Cosmo?"

Shelly keeps walking, looking straight ahead. "I think you've had enough."

I know she's not twenty-one, because I remember her birthday episode on TV and I was excited we were almost the same age. From what I've seen on the tabloid covers, being rich gets you special privileges.

Kiki rolls her eyes. "You *always* say that and I *always* tell you *I'm not driving myself home* so it doesn't matter how much I have!"

Shelly looks over her shoulder. "I still think you've had

enough," she insists. "Why don't you go home and sleep it off. . . ." She glares at Gabe. "Alone."

Gabe laughs and puts an arm around Kiki. "I'll have a beer while you're at it—twenty-two ounce. You're buying, right, babe?"

"Sure!" Kiki says loudly. She scans the room and then zeroes in on me. "You," she says, pointing in my direction. "I don't know you, but I'll buy you one too." She reaches into a micro-mini handbag and takes out a fistful of crumpled cash. "Whadda ya want?"

I shake my head. "Um, I'm good."

Kiki laughs and throws the bills on the pool table. "Oh, my God, you're turning down *free* booze? What planet are you from? Get our drinks will you?" she says to Gabe, pushing him in the direction of the bar. She jumps from the pool table, tugs her skirt, and then plops herself down in the chair opposite me. "Do you know who I am?" she asks, swinging an arm out and knocking my beer over.

I push my chair back and grab some napkins as beer starts to pour onto my lap. "Geez!"

Kiki giggles. "Sorry. I'll buy you another, but do you know who I am?"

I stare across the table hardly believing this is the same girl I used to love to watch on TV. "No, I don't. And I have to go." I turn my back to her and take my wallet out from my bag, careful not to expose the two stakes inside.

"Do *The Disco Unicorns* mean anything to you?"

"No," I say putting some money down on the table.

Kiki gives me an incredulous look. "Multiplatinum, kiddie-rock band?"

"Sorry." I sling my purse strap over my shoulder and head for the door.

"TV show on the Kidz Network?" she asks, following me. "Still in production."

"Doesn't sound familiar." I wind my way around the tables and then open the door, praying she won't come after me. I just want to find Mom and Dad and see if we got the job—although at this point I'm hoping Mr. Harker made a better impression and we can move on.

Kiki follows me out. "Cut the shit. *Everyone* knows The Disco Unicorns." She looks up at me and taps her foot impatiently on the sidewalk while humming the tune to "Puppy Parade."

Why me?

Folding my arms across my chest I say the first thing that comes to mind that might get Kiki Crusher out of my face. "Oh, wait," I say as if the idea has just come to me. "Isn't that the band *Sugar LeBlanc* sings with?"

Kiki's eyes widen and she takes a few steps backward.

"You're fucking kidding me, right? That bitch can't *sing* for shit!"

She looks really upset and I remind myself that just because I don't have a life doesn't mean I have to take it out on innocent bystanders—no matter how trashy they are. "Sorry, *Maybelle*, but if it makes you feel better I always thought you were way better than Sugar and her deranged *Joker* smile."

She doubles over laughing and grabs a street sign post to keep from falling. "Ha! I *knew* you recognized me." She looks conspiratorially around and then brings a finger to her lips. "Shhhh. Let me tell you a secret. . . . What's your name?"

"Daphne. Daphne Van Helsing."

She laughs again—like my name is any stupider than either one of hers. "Well, *Daphne*, Sugar LeBitch lip-synched to a blend of both of our vocals. Hers weren't good enough to go it alone, but don't tell anyone or the record label will send a hit man after us."

Despite all the things I've seen and heard in my life I still find this shocking news. "But why wouldn't you just do the singing? I mean, your parents are the lead singers!"

She seems to deflate on the spot. "The producers didn't think I was photogenic enough. And long story short, my parents agreed." She runs her fingers through her hair and takes another step back. "You know what—I'm not feeling so good. I think I should go home."

"What about your friend inside?"

"Eh, I don't feel like dealing with him with tonight—he never calls afterward anyway." She shakes her head. "Asshole." Kiki takes one more step back and goes over the curb, landing on her butt in the street. "Shit! Shit! Shit!" she mutters as I rush over to help her up.

I pull her back to her feet and she pushes me away. "I'm *fine*! I don't need any help!"

"You're bleeding," I say eyeing her elbow. Drops of blood well up where her skin scraped the pavement. I do a quick scan up and down the street. If South Bristol is attracting vamps it's most likely newbies who are ravenous and Kiki Crusher is now chum. I reach into my purse and put one hand on a stake. "Let me walk you out."

She cradles her elbow with one hand and shakes her head. "You don't have to. I don't even know why I came out after you. Too much to drink, I guess."

She heads toward the alleyway and this time I'm following her. I have to make sure she gets to her car okay. "Um, tell me more about Sugar." As soon as the words leave my mouth I wish I'd thought of something less painful to ask about. God, my social skills are abysmal, but it's not like I've had much opportunity to fine-tune them.

Kiki stops and looks back at me. "Sugar was dimples and blue eyes, and I was big-nose, mousy hair, and weight issues. Having craft services laying out all that junk food on set every day didn't help with that. But the advertisers said kids weren't buying my action figure because I was chubby, and a focus group concluded a cuter kid would boost sales."

She stops and tilts her chin up to the sky. "I can sing rings around Sugar, but they put *her* center stage and I got stuck dancing backup in a unicorn costume." She looks at me. "Do you know how hard it was to watch Sugar playing it up with my parents on the red carpet or photo shoots like she was their kid? They don't usually televise the kids' CD winner at the Grammys, but the year they put Sugar in the band they turned into superstars and got a prime-time slot. I was five years old and I was in the background."

"Wow."

"Yeah," Kiki whispers. "It sucked watching Sugar being a shiny, prettier version of me."

On the scale of suckiness that is definitely up there.

She leans over and rests her hands on her bent knees. "Did I also tell you I don't feel so good?" She starts to rock on her feet and I remember the goal is to get her off the streets.

"Let me help you to your car."

She nods and I put an arm around her.

"Uh-oh," she says again, putting her hand to her mouth. "Hold on." She leans over and I cringe as she throws up a liquid brown mess that reeks of alcohol and bile. She coughs and spits, and then looks up at me as she wipes her mouth. "Sorry."

"It's okay." What else can I say? "Come on, we're almost there." The driver's leaning his head against the window and I'm guessing he's fallen asleep.

I open the back door and Kiki stumbles in. She leans forward and taps the man on the shoulder. "Sam, I'm ready."

A woman with a bloodstained face pops up beside the driver and Kiki screams, *"Who the hell are you?"*

The woman pushes the driver away and he moans and grabs the steering wheel to steady himself. Blood drips from two wounds on his neck.

Kiki's mouth drops open. "Sam? Are you okay?"

From the dim light hanging by the back door of the pub I can just make out the fangs as the vampire starts to scramble over the seat toward Kiki.

Kiki lets out another horror-movie scream, and I drag her out of the car. "Run! Go back in the bar—don't come out until I tell you to!"

"That bitch was eating my bodyguard!"

"Just run!" I shriek, pushing her in the direction of the front door.

I pull a stake out of my bag as the vampire crawls into the backseat. She eyes me hungrily with glowing black eyes. Her body tenses and then she lunges out of the car like a panther, knocking me to the ground. My head slams into the pavement and I try to blink away the pain.

A mouth full of teeth growls over me and with a snarl she dives in toward my neck. I smell the metallic-tasting blood in her mouth and suddenly a pointed boot arcs inches from my face and connects with the vampire's chin, knocking her off me.

I roll toward her across the pavement, gravel digging into my hands and knuckles, and then grunt as I plunge the stake in her chest.

"Shit!" I've missed the mark by a long shot—there was no sound of bones cracking to tell me I'd broken through the ribs. Her mouth opens in a silent scream as her hands claw at the stake. My near miss hasn't done a thing to dampen her fight.

"Damn it," I mutter through gritted teeth. I punch the woman in the face to distract her, then straddle her and yank the stake out. She bares her teeth like a wild animal and lifts her head toward me as I drive the stake back in. Her clawlike fingers ball up in fists as her dark eyes widen. Her arms fall to her sides and her body stills like she's suddenly fallen asleep. Blood puddles up out of her mouth and trickles from her nose. I pull out the knife from the sheath strapped to my calf. It takes three strokes but I finally sever her head and knock it away from her body with the blade.

I spy my purse across the pavement and hustle to it. Once a vamp has been exterminated it's urgent the authorities are notified for pickup to avoid people stumbling onto the scene. I fumble for my cell phone and call Mom.

One ring, two—

"Daphne?"

"Mom! I just staked a vamp," I say breathlessly. "We'll need body removal, and there's a victim. He appears to be okay, I'm thinking the vampire hadn't been at it long. I'm behind The Rusty Rudder."

"Any witnesses?" she asks.

My stomach drops. The boot. I look toward the car and Kiki Crusher is hovering over her driver, who is assuring her he's okay.

She turns to me with wild, excited eyes. "That was freaking *epic*!"

4. "Daphne, are you still there?"

I redirect my attention to the phone. "Uh, sorry, beside the vic, there's one witness."

Mom sighs. "Just what I was hoping to avoid; that's going to cost us. We agreed to let them dock our pay if there are witnesses."

Crap. "Sorry."

"It's okay, I'm sure it was unavoidable," she says with a hint of annoyance in her voice. "Is the witness doing okay? Should I tell the agents to have a tranquilizer ready?"

Kiki is still staring at me, shaking her head and smiling crazily. "No, she doesn't appear to need sedation; she seems to be handling the whole thing remarkably well."

"Good, maybe the town can convince her to take a lesser payment for keeping mum. I'll tell them to lowball her in negotiations and as soon as I contact the removal crew we'll head over. See if you can at least get the body out of the way so it won't be seen by anyone else."

"Okay."

I shut my phone and my shoulders slump. "Any chance you can just pretend this didn't happen?" I ask.

Kiki laughs hysterically. "Are you on crack? You just freaking staked and cut the head off what looked like an honest to God *vampire* and you think I'm going to pretend it didn't happen?" She laughs some more and throws her arms in the air. "I've never seen anything like that in my life. I feel like I've been sleeping for a hundred years and all of sudden I woke up. Wow!"

"Don't get too excited. It's just the adrenaline pumping through your system; it temporarily negates the effect of all the alcohol you consumed. The booze will hit you again soon and hopefully you'll forget all about this."

"No way; I was *meant* to see this—it's like destiny. And since you came prepared," she says, pointing to the stake protruding from the woman's heart, "I'm assuming this isn't the first time you've done this."

"I've lost count, actually."

"Incredible. You're an *actual* vampire slayer." She

circles the body and then looks at me. "Wait, you said your last name was Van Helsing? As in the guy who killed Dracula?"

"He didn't actually kill Dracula—he just kind of supervised."

"Wow," she says again. "I don't know where to begin. I have, like, a gazillion questions to ask you, but the big one is . . ." She pulls me away from the car. "Is Sam going to turn into a vampire?" she whispers. "And if so, how much time does he have left?"

"He's okay," I assure her. "To get turned you'd have to have your blood completely drained and left for dead. The corpse then reanimates the following night. Morticians always look for bite marks so they won't be taken by surprise."

She laughs. "Phew! That's a huge relief. *You're cool, Sam,*" she calls out. "Did you get a bandage from the first-aid kit?"

"Yes, Miss Crusher."

"Your neck okay?"

He gives her the thumbs-up.

She turns back to me. "He's so badass—if only he wasn't like thirty—and gay—I'd be all over him. But we were a little worried. I mean besides being, like, *undead,* my parents would've probably found some way to blame me. '*If only you had stayed with the band and not run off to the summer cottage, Sam wouldn't be a vampire,*'" she says in a high-pitched voice. "Good help is hard to come by, but they'd write me out of their will if *that* happened."

It's obvious Kiki Crusher is living on a very different planet than mine.

She looks down at the body. "Are they all crazed like that or do some of them have it together enough to, like, go out with?"

"Go out with?"

"Yeah, you know, like on a date." She looks at me hopefully. "In books vampires are all really romantic. Wouldn't you just die to hear '*Daphne, I've been waiting a hundred years for a girl like you to come into my life,*'" she says with some sort of foreign accent. She fans her face. "*It'd be so hot.*"

I can't believe I'm having this conversation. I point a finger at the corpse. "Did that look like someone *anybody* would want to date?"

Kiki appraises the body parts. "Well, she looked better before you cut her head off, but maybe she was just really cranky because we interrupted her," Kiki says hopefully. "Or maybe she was just having an off night."

"She's a vampire—*all* her nights were off!"

Kiki sticks her lip out in a pout. "They can't all be bad."

"I probably shouldn't tell you this, but there are *older*

vampires who survive the need-to-feed-twenty-four-seven early stage. They pretty much keep to themselves so they don't get staked." I raise an eyebrow. "And there are plenty of *weirdos* with vampire fetishes who don't mind sharing their blood, if you get my drift."

She pumps a fist in the air. "Then there's hope!"

"Why would you want to date someone who drinks blood and is short a soul? I mean *really*?"

Kiki's eyes fill with disappointment. "But I always imagined older vampires would have this maturity that allows them to appreciate a good woman. Unlike assholes like Gabe."

I reach out and touch the knot on the back of my head and wince. As the adrenaline in my own body wanes, my scraped knuckles sting and my fingers ache from the death grip I used on the stake. A dull twinge pulses in my right shoulder, but there's no rest for the weary. "As much as I'd love to chat about why dating a vampire might very well be better than hooking up with Gabe, I need to move the body before anyone else sees it."

I survey the torso and head lying nearby—it looks like she was middle-aged and nicely dressed. Not a typical homeless-person-turned-vamp which are usually the first to go when places get infested. But maybe a summer resort town like this is low on homeless people. Some vamp probably got her to open the door to her house and wrangled an invitation in.

I grab an arm and start to drag the corpse back by the Dumpster. Kiki grabs the other arm and joins me. I stop and stare at her in disbelief.

"I've never been squeamish," she says.

"Yeah, I'm getting that."

She continues pulling so I keep going.

Kiki stumbles a bit. "Damn heels."

I almost laugh—I could've told her hunting in heels is a bad idea.

The body gets caught on a snag in the pavement and we tug harder. "She's heavier than she looks," Kiki says. "And I thought there'd be more blood."

"Since she wasn't alive her blood doesn't pump like ours, so no big spurt like in the horror movies. If I had staked her in the stomach there would've been more— depending on how much she'd fed."

We move the body around the side of the Dumpster and my nose wrinkles as I inhale the rotting food.

Kiki wipes her brow. "Is there, like, an *army* of vampires trying to kill mankind I should be worried about?"

I give her a sideways look. "No. For the most part they just have outbreaks here and there—like the flu. Generally, vampires are solitary, but sometimes they get lonely — especially the new ones — and they make a 'friend' not realizing the newbie vamp will be competing with them for blood. More bodies mean you're more likely to get noticed."

Kiki nods. "Why didn't she turn to dust?"

"Only a really, really old vamp would do that. Once you stake them the process of decay accelerates to the point it would have been at if the body wasn't in a state of vampiric suspended animation of sorts. So ninety-nine-point-nine percent of the time there is some sort of body to dispose of."

I go back and pick the head up by the hair and shiver. Cutting off heads is the easy part — it's picking them up afterward that still gets me. I hold the head out at arm's length to avoid the blood slowly dripping from the neck and mouth. "Since you have such a strong stomach you can get the head next time," I joke, placing it gently on the ground a few feet away from the body.

"Do you have superpowers?"

A laugh escapes my mouth. "Superpowers?"

She nods. "Yeah, are you, like, *a chosen one* or part of a superior race of people who have special powers to help you fight vampires and save the world?"

She makes staking vampires sound almost noble. "No, I just come from a crazy family who for reasons beyond my comprehension decided to exterminate the undead instead of holding down nine-to-five jobs. Actually, my dad's family has been doing this for a couple of hundred years, but why my mother joined the fray is a complete mystery. She refuses to talk about it and I've given up asking."

"Wow." Kiki looks down at the body and then back up at me. "This is so awesome. I cannot believe I'm really going to hunt vampires with you!" She shakes her fists, and lets out a squeal.

My stomach flips. "What? Who said anything about hunting vampires with me?"

"You did. You said next time *I* could pick up the head."

"I was kidding when I said that. And besides, who ever heard of a vampire slayer named *Kiki*?"

"Well, it's a lot better than a slayer named Maybelle. And I think Kiki *Crusher* is very slayerish," she says, wiggling her fingers in the air for emphasis.

I roll my eyes. "There is nothing slayerish about jazz hands."

She puts a hand on one hip. "Yeah, well, *Daphne* doesn't exactly scream slayer either."

"Touché."

We stare at each other for a few seconds and then Kiki looks down at the head. "Why *did* you cut it off by the way?"

"If the head reconnects with the body the vampire can come back to life. Oh . . ." I walk over to my purse and pull out a garlic bulb and then stuff it in the vampire's mouth, careful to avoid cutting my fingers on the fangs. "You're supposed to use garlic, too."

Kiki eyes the corpse. "If the head is already you know—*decapitated*—why bother with the garlic? And do you really think it would *reattach*? Seems like a bit of a stretch to me."

"A bit of a stretch?" I gasp, glaring at her.

"Have you actually seen that happen?"

"Well, no," I admit. "But slayers have been following up staking with decapitation and garlic for hundreds of years."

Kiki scoffs. "People did a lot of boneheaded stuff hundreds of years ago, but it's the twenty-first century now. A million bucks says the head won't reattach itself even if you glued it back on."

"Oh, and you feel safe with this bet because of your vast experience with severed vampire heads?"

She points to the torso. "It's not like a vampire with a stake through its heart is going to pick up its head, place it on its neck and then '*alakazam!*' they're back to life. And really, how would a decapitated vampire even *find* its head?"

I stare at the body and have to admit it does sound a little far-fetched—but I remind myself the same can be said for vampires. "I was told it could happen and just the fact that there are undead creatures living on blood shows there is some pretty freaky stuff in the world, and I for one am not ruling out that the heads can reattach themselves."

Still, I make a mental note to ask Mom and Dad about this.

Kiki laughs. "Whatever. I'm not buying it."

My upper lip curls up in annoyance. "And how many vampires have *you* killed?" I ask, echoing my mother's earlier question to Officer MacCready.

She puts her hands on her hips defiantly. "None *yet*, but if we were attacked by, like, a whole army of vampires I'd think we'd either want to cut off their heads *or* stake them—doing both would be redundant and bending over and putting garlic in their mouths is just asking to get ambushed from behind." She fingers the top of the stake sticking out of the woman's chest. "Don't you think this pretty much does the trick?"

"No!" I say defiantly, as I pull the stake out.

"Well, if it's all the same to you I think I'll be a *rebel* slayer." She punctuates this statement with more jazz hands. "I'll just use stakes as my primary method of slaying. If you still want to cut the heads off I won't hold it against you—unless we were in that vampire army scenario. Then I'd insist you pick one method or the other because time would be of the essence."

I throw my hands up in the air. "This is ridiculous. There is no *vampire army* and even if there were I highly doubt your skills as a singer-slash-backup-dancer qualify you to hunt *squirrels*, let alone an army of the undead."

"Hello? Is someone forgetting that I clocked that vamp—maybe even saving your life—with a well-placed high kick?"

"I could've easily gotten her off me." I decide not to admit that having a vampire on top is probably the worst position to be in because they're so damn strong.

Kiki laughs. "Yeah, I'm sure you were seconds away from getting the upper hand, but I also took tae kwon do for a year when I was ten and Master Kandro said I was a natural."

"And this qualifies you to hunt vampires *how*?"

Kiki spins and then kicks up. The tip of one of her boots sails a fraction of an inch from my chin. A spray of dirt from the bottom of her shoe hits my face and I jump back away from her. *"Are you completely nuts?"*

She loses her balance and crashes to the pavement again. "Crap!"

I wipe my face with my sleeve. *"What the hell are you doing?"*

She slowly pushes herself up. "Showing you what a year of tae kwon do could do to a vampire. If you had been one—and I hadn't landed on my ass—I would've just knocked you to the ground and you'd have a stake sticking out of your chest." She brushes her hands like it would've been as easy as driving a pen through a piece of paper. "By the way, do all the stakes look like this? It's a little big—like a fence post. I think a trimmer model might be more fashion forward, don't you?"

Usually at this point I'd be consoling the witnesses until the police arrive, but Kiki Crusher is acting like killing vamps is the next big craze complete with "fashion forward" accessories. "Do you even have a clue how much strength it takes to get a stake through a rib cage?" I say finally. "I am constantly working out and it's still hard to do."

"I did notice it took you two tries to get it in." She curls up her arm and makes a muscle. "But I work out too. I know I could do it if you show me how."

Dear God, I've officially had it. I am standing by a Dumpster reeking of rotting food. The back of my head is throbbing, and my body aches. My mother will be here any second, pissed off that I killed the vampire in front of a witness. Officer MacCready will be pissed the town will have to pay her and the driver, and I'm pissed Kiki thinks this lame existence of mine is something to be envied.

"Look, you and I are *never* going to hunt vampires together. *Not going to happen!*"

Kiki's brow furrows and she bites her lip. "Why? Is there some super-secret slayer society? Sign me up; I'll pay the dues."

"It's just easier to hunt alone."

"But I could help you."

I shake my head. "This is a *dangerous* business."

"I don't care," she insists.

Why won't she take no for an answer? I put my hands on my hips. "Okay, to be completely honest, I'm pretty sure you have a *drinking* problem, therefore making you a huge liability. Simply put, I'm not risking my life for some bored little rich kid. This is serious stuff, and definitely *not* for amateurs."

"Jeez," she says quietly. "I just wanted to help." She rubs her backside where she landed on the ground. "And I *don't* have a drinking problem—not every night, anyway. I would never drink on the job."

"Look, the police are going to arrive any second—"

Her eyes widen. "The police know about vampires too?"

"Yes," I say wearily, as my temple starts to throb. "A lot of people know about them, but it's kept quiet because it would cause mass panic, cripple the restaurant and entertainment industries, and it's not something the government wants to make common knowledge. Nine out of ten people will never even encounter a vampire."

"Wow, this is just like the Area 51 conspiracy, only with vampires. Cool."

I'm still having trouble fathoming what she thinks is so cool about this whole thing, but it's clear she's completely deranged. "Look, the vampire task force for South Bristol will take you and your driver to the station and negotiate a fee so you can be in on the *conspiracy* while keeping your mouth shut. Cool, right?"

Kiki nibbles her lip and wobbles a little—the alcohol's obviously hitting her again. "Does paying people even really work? You'd think the tabloids would be paying bigger bucks than the government ever would."

I look her in the eye. "If you don't take the money, they kind of imply they'll ruin you. As in you just *disappear*."

She shakes her head. "That's fucked-up. But they don't need to pay me. The last thing I need is *'washed-up child star says driver was attacked by an army of vampires—news at eleven.'*"

"*Please* stop saying 'army of vampires,'" I beg.

"Sorry," she snaps. "I didn't grow up hunting vampires so I don't know everything like you do. I didn't realize this was such an elitist profession."

I squeeze my eyes shut and, for the hundredth time,

wonder what planet Kiki Crusher is from. "Killing vampires is not fun, cool, or fashionable. It just honest to God sucks!"

She looks toward the car at her driver. "Maybe it's not *fun* or *cool*, but it is important. Without you, Sam and I might be dead—or undead."

I hear a noisy muffler come up the alley and I'm relieved to see Mom and Dad pulling up in the van. A white hearselike car follows them and I figure that must be the South Bristol vamp squad.

Mom and Dad get out and look at Kiki as if she's some sort of wounded fawn. "Are you okay, Miss?" Dad asks gently.

"I know this must have been quite a shock," Mom says, reaching out a hand to pat Kiki's shoulder. "You're a very brave girl."

Mom's laying it on thick—anything to keep us from looking bad during the negotiations.

Two men with buzz cuts get out of the white car and march toward us. They're wearing dark suits and no-nonsense attitudes. While Mom is trying to butter Kiki up, they'll use the opposite technique and try to stay completely emotionless and avoid saying anything that might upset her more. Two men in hazmat suits get out of the back—the cleanup crew. I tilt my head toward the Dumpster so they can pick up the body.

Dad points to me. "Agents, this is our daughter, Daphne. And this courageous young lady here is the one who witnessed the attack."

"I'm Special Task Force Agent Sloan," the tall one says shaking Kiki's hand. "You'll need to come down to the station. We have a counselor waiting to help you deal with this . . . *event*."

I roll my eyes. I've never heard a member of a vampire task force actually use the word "vampire."

Kiki looks back and forth between my parents and Agent Sloan. I wait for her to tell them she's fine, but then her bottom lip quivers and all of a sudden she's sobbing uncontrollably. I'm stunned to see actual tears streaming down her cheeks.

"It was so *horrible*," she wails. "I thought my driver was going to *die* and then I'd be next. *This will haunt me for the rest of my life!*"

5.

Kiki takes in a blubbery gulp of air and my father puts an arm around her.

"It's okay, honey," he coos. "Take a deep breath."

"What are you doing?" I ask Kiki.

She ignores me and keeps her tirade going. "I thought the worst was over but then"—Kiki jabs a finger in my direction—"*she* cut the woman's head off! She even held it up and"—her voice quivers—"and said I could pick up the *next one*."

"Daphne!" Mom snaps. "What were you thinking?"

My mouth drops open as adrenaline pumps through my system again. "It's not like it sounds. She was totally fine a minute ago. *Tell them you're fine, Kiki*. Tell them how you're not squeamish."

Mom glares at me as Kiki howls.

"She was *fine* until you showed up," I insist. "She even helped me drag the body behind the Dumpster."

Kiki buries her head on Dad's chest. "I thought she might be some sort of psycho killer and I was afraid if I didn't help her she might stake me next."

"She's lying!" I shout. "She thought the whole thing was totally *cool*. She even went on and on about how she'd fight an army of vampires!"

Kiki lifts her head from Dad's chest and slowly turns toward me, gasping dramatically. She puts a hand to her mouth and takes in a ragged breath. "There are *armies of vampires*?"

Dear God.

The other agent shakes his head and frowns at me. Then he clears his throat and marches over to Kiki. "I'm Agent Brennan. I think you need to talk with our event specialist, Katie Anthony. Ms. Anthony can help you process whatever emotions you might be feeling."

Kiki grabs his arm, shaking it frantically. "There's no time," she says pulling him toward the cars. "We have to alert the media and tell the world that *vampires are real*!"

Officer Sloan groans and I imagine he's thinking this is going to cost the town big-time. "Now, Miss, let's not get carried away. Come with us to the station," he says gently. "Brennan, you get the driver."

Kiki nods and lets him escort her to the car. Before they take more than three steps she pulls away.

"Wait!" She stands up straight, sniffs delicately, and places a hand over her heart like she's about to recite the Pledge of Allegiance. "I have just had an *epiphany*." She stares off into the night for a few seconds, and then turns to look us each in the eye. Her face transforms from one filled with terror to that of a stalwart soldier. "If there really are vampire armies out there, someone needs to fight them. Why couldn't that someone be *me*?"

Agent Brennan's eyes widen. "Miss?"

"Here's the deal," Kiki says matter-of-factly. "If Daphne here teaches me the ins and outs of killing vampires you won't have to pay me any hush money."

Mom clenches her jaw and looks disbelievingly at me. "You told her about the money?"

I bury my head in my hands.

Kiki folds her arms across her very large chest. "She did, but I'd be willing to forgo any compensation for my *harrowing* ordeal if she agrees to show me the ropes."

Mom nods. "She'll do it."

"No, I won't!" I say. "Don't you get it—this is all an *act*."

Kiki shrugs. "I guess we'll have to head to the station and discuss money, then. I'll have to call my parents and their team of lawyers first. You do know my parents, don't you? *The Crushers*—lead singers of The Disco Unicorns? Name above the library door? Part of a billion-dollar media empire that could destroy this town with a clack of their little pink hooves? They're going to be pretty upset to hear vampires have moved in around our cottage and how this traumatic near-death experience will no doubt affect my mental health."

"Good lord," Agent Brennan mutters, exchanging a look with Agent Sloan. "The Crushers."

"Miss Crusher," Dad says softly. "Daphne would be happy to show you 'the ropes' in exchange for not collecting a fee."

"Dad," I whine. "Do you really think it's safe bringing a novice on jobs?"

Mom pulls me aside. "Daphne," she says through clenched teeth. "We need the money *and* the goodwill of the police department. Having the Harkers here has completely turned the game around. Besides, how long do you think a girl like that is going to last anyway?"

I look at Kiki in her high heel boots and a micro-mini so short I know *Jennifer-Kate* would put her on the "Fashion Faux Pas" page at the back of the magazine.

Mom's right. Kiki won't last a day.

"Fine, she can shadow me tomorrow—and however long it takes until the town is clean."

Kiki beams and claps her hands. "I promise I won't get in the way. And even though I don't think it's necessary, I will slice and dice heads if that's what you tell me to do."

"You'll just be observing," I insist.

"Okay." She turns to the agents. "So, is there, like, some form or something I need to sign releasing the town from liability and swearing me to secrecy?" she asks nonchalantly.

Agent Sloan's face is a mix of relief and confusion. "Uh, yes, if you wouldn't mind." He turns to look at her car. "About your driver?"

She waves a hand dismissively in the air. "I'll give him a raise; it won't cost you a thing."

Agent Sloan exchanges a quick look with Agent Brennan and I know they're thinking they lucked out with Kiki.

"We will have to contact your parents, though," Agent Brennan says.

She shakes her head. "I'm an emancipated minor so they don't have to know anything."

If the agents weren't trying so hard to play it cool, I'd bet they'd be high-fiving each other right about now.

"We'll follow you to the station in my car. Sam, are you good to drive?"

"Yes, Miss Crusher," he calls out.

Kiki smiles at all of us. "It's settled, then." She turns to me. "So, what time should we meet tomorrow?"

"Six a.m. will be fine," Mom says. "That will give Daphne time to brief you and give some rudimentary instruction before we start house cleaning."

I smirk and suppress a laugh. *Go, Mom!*

Kiki grimaces. "Six? That's a little early. I usually don't get up before eleven. And what is this about house-cleaning? I thought we were hunting vampires."

"'House cleaning' is a euphemism for killing vampires in their lairs—or in this town, their vacation homes," I tell her. "Vampires are less powerful during the day and easier to dispatch. How big of a list do we have?" I ask my parents.

Dad walks over to the van and opens the driver's door. He leans in and pulls out a folder. He opens it as he comes back our way. "We have ten houses identified for possible cleaning."

"We'll definitely have to split up because the Harkers are *sharing* the job with us," Mom says, not bothering to hide the disgust in her voice.

My mouth drops open again. "No way! We're sharing the job? How does that even work?"

Mom scowls. "We've agreed to forgo our usual fee. Instead, we'll get paid for each vampire killed. If the

Harkers beat us to the punch, we're out of luck. But there are three of us and only two of them."

Kiki raises her hand. "Four!"

"You'll be in training," I say without enthusiasm. "So that still counts as three."

"We've also agreed to take a pay cut for every witness, but there is a five-thousand-dollar bonus for whichever 'team' can get a definitive answer as to why the influx of vampires has coincided with whatever is preying on the kids."

"What's wrong with praying for kids?" Kiki asks.

"*Preying on*—as in hunting," I say. "Something is sending kids to the hospital and it started around the same time the vamps arrived."

"We're staying at the Water's Edge Economy Lodge on West Side Road," Mom continues. "We have only one vehicle so you'll have to use your own transportation—is that a problem, Ms. Crusher?"

Kiki frowns, no doubt still thinking about the early morning wake-up call she'll need. "No, Sam can drive me. I kind of lost my license—but I was only over the limit by like a fraction of a point. There was also the underage thing." She shrugs and I can't believe she's telling us she has a DWI on her record.

"Are you ready, Miss?" Agent Brennan asks her.

She nods and he leads her to her car. He opens the door for her and she turns to wave to me. "See you tomorrow." She rolls her eyes and laughs. "Bright and early."

As the pink car backs out of the alley I shake my head. This is a disaster waiting to happen.

The hotel sign is glowing in the dark ahead and I wish Dad would drive faster. I can't wait to get in my own room and be alone.

Agent Sloan phoned to warn me that I better do a good job so Kiki doesn't call up that "team of lawyers" and have them figure out a way to null and void the contract she'd signed.

Why couldn't the police have just awarded this gig to the Harkers? I still can't believe my parents agree to share the job. I know the van needs a new muffler, but still.

"How am I supposed to hunt when I have that girl with me?" I lament. "And what if she gets bitten or something?"

Mom turns around to face me. "You're hunting during the day when the vampires are almost powerless."

"I guess, but what if she wants to go on night patrol with me?"

"I don't think that's going to be an issue."

I think about Kiki saying she wasn't squeamish. "I hope you're right."

Dad pulls into a parking spot and I watch an assortment of insects flit in and around the lights illuminating the one level, no-frills motel. Faded plastic flowers droop in the window boxes and I eye the soda machine under an awning near the office. I'm going to need caffeine in the morning and this doesn't look like the kind of place that will have a coffeemaker and packets of instant in the bathroom.

"This just might be good for you, Doodlebug. Living like we do doesn't leave much time for friends."

"Much time? How about *no* time?" And Kiki Crusher would be the last person I'd pick to be friends with. I scowl just thinking about her. "And even if I did want to be friends with her, we'll be gone in a week's time so what would the point be?"

"This isn't about making friends," Mom says gathering her things. "It's about getting the job done no matter what obstacles they throw in our way. And like I said, I'd bet money that girl will be out of your hair in less than twenty-four hours."

Suddenly Mom slaps the dashboard and I jump. "Oh, great, figures *they're* here."

I scan the lot. Mr. Harker is leaning on a rusted blue car smoking a cigarette. He sees us looking at him and nods.

Mom practically growls. "He's infuriating."

"Joy, it hasn't been easy for him," Dad says gently. "I really think he's sincere in wanting to reconnect."

"That's never going to happen," Mom whispers. "Never." She shakes her head. "If he hadn't been so reckless—hadn't encouraged her to follow suit—she'd still be here." Mom takes in a long breath.

I shift uncomfortably in the back. It occurs to me that Mom must have been friends with Mrs. Harker, and like Dad implied, friends are hard to come by. I'm having a hard time picturing Mom relaxing and laughing with a friend, though—she's always so serious. But maybe there was a time. . . .

"I know you still miss her . . . ," Dad starts.

Mom sits up straight, game face back on. "Let's check in. We have a lot of planning and research to do if we want to come out ahead." She puts her purse strap over her shoulder and opens her door. "I'll get the keys." She slams the door harder than necessary and stalks toward the hotel office.

I steal a look at Mr. Harker and I wonder if Dad misses working with him. I imagine he was a different man before he had to stake his wife. His face is heavily lined and with the greasy, thinning hair and unkempt clothes it's clear the years haven't been kind to him. He takes a drag on his cigarette and his head turns to follow Mom as she makes her way to the office.

I catch Dad peeking at Mr. Harker too. "How long did you work together?" I ask.

Dad looks away. "Since we were boys. Our parents worked together too. Our mothers watched us in shifts. I always assumed we'd do the same until . . ."

He doesn't finish his sentence but I know what he's thinking—until Mrs. Harker got turned; reason number one million and one of why this business sucks.

"Let's get settled," Dad says, opening his door. "We have a lot of ground to cover before Ms. Crusher joins us in the morning."

I grab my crate and bump the door closed with my hip. The hotel stands by itself by the side of the road, one long single-story building wrapped in a blanket of night sky. I can't help but notice the clarity of the stars—so different from Buffalo where we'd just been.

Mom comes out of the office looking straight ahead, obviously trying to avoid eye contact with Mr. Harker.

"Joy," Mr. Harker calls out loudly. "Do you have a minute?"

Mom visibly stiffens as he walks toward her. "I have nothing to say to you, Nathan," she replies coldly as she keeps going.

He throws his cigarette down and crushes it with his heavy boot and then hurries to catch up with her. "I just want to apologize again," he says. "I was out of line talking to Officer MacCready about Vince's father—way out of line. But I think us working together like this is fate. It's been too long; it's time to mend fences."

She stops and turns, pointing a finger in his face. "You threw us under the bus!" she hisses.

"Wait here," Dad says, coming around the van. I honestly think Dad would give Mr. Harker a second chance, but Mom wears the pants in this family. He hustles over to Mom and puts an arm protectively around her shoulder. "Nathan, now is not a good time. Give us a chance to process everything."

Mom stares incredulously at Dad. "There is nothing to process! We had an agreement." She turns to Mr. Harker, eyes blazing. "You would stay on the West Coast and we would work the East. It was the perfect arrangement. What are you even *doing* here, Nathan?"

Mr. Harker runs his fingers through his greasy hair and then looks a bit wildly around the parking lot as if he's expecting something to jump out at them. "It's time. Can't you feel it?" His eyes dart around some more as he fidgets with the ring on his hand. "I've been waiting so long," he mutters. He looks at Dad hopefully. "But something told me I had to come east. And meeting up with you—here in this town—it was meant to be. Tell me you can't feel it."

Mom and Dad exchange looks and I'm sure they're thinking the same thing I am: Mr. Harker is nuts.

"We can work together," he insists. "I know things—dark things," he says quietly. "It can be like it used to."

Mom's eyes widen and she looks almost afraid of Mr. Harker. "I don't know what you're talking about and I don't want to know. Just stay away from my family, and when this job is over I want you to get the hell back to the West Coast and keep out of our territory."

Mr. Harker's lips turn up into a slight smile. "You just need some time to get used to the idea. It always did take you time to warm up to things." He looks at Dad and winks. "She'll come around." He laughs. "She always does. Right, Vince?"

A door opens and Tyler Harker pokes his head out of his room. "Dad, *come inside.*"

The tone of his voice makes it clear he's embarrassed. I imagine he's been watching the scene from his room.

Mr. Harker ignores Tyler. "And think about my boy. He needs people in his life, people who understand what we do. So does your girl."

Dad purses his lips. He glances at Mom, who shakes her head ever so slightly. "It's not going to work, Nathan," he says. "I'm sorry." He leads Mom back toward the van.

"Dad, come on!" From the light pouring out of his room I can see that Tyler's hair is slicked back from being in the shower. I wonder if this is the first hotel he's stayed at in a while—the first shower.

"It's fate!" Mr. Harker calls out. "You can't fight it any more than I can. *The die has been cast.*"

As he says this, a shiver runs through me. Mom reaches the van, grabs my arm roughly, and pulls me toward our rooms. "Let's go, Daphne." She looks over her shoulder at Mr. Harker and hustles me along.

She sticks the card in the door for room fourteen and the lock whirs and clicks. The green light comes on and Dad opens the door and ushers us in. The air is fairly stale inside. They must not get a lot of people this time of year. I put my crate on the small desk and see there's no adjoining door, so I'll have a little more privacy without Mom barging in whenever she feels like it.

Mom sits on one of the twin beds and starts obsessively picking at the fuzzballs on the ugly brown and pink floral patterned bedspread. "He's crazy. I can't believe Officer MacCready didn't take one look at Nathan and toss him out of his office." She stares up at the ceiling and shakes her head. "And demons, of all things!"

This gets my attention. "Demons? What are you talking about?"

Mom gets up and paces in the small room. "He went on and on about demons being responsible for the attacks on the children and Officer MacCready acted like that was a credible theory. *'There're vampires, why not demons,'*" she says, obviously recounting what Officer MacCready said in his office after I'd left.

"What kind of demons?" I ask.

"He didn't get into the details," Dad says. "He wanted to talk to us afterward but we—"

"We said 'no' of course," Mom interrupts. "You need to stay away from them, Daphne."

I roll my eyes. "You won't get any arguments from me."

"God, this job can't end soon enough," she mutters.

"Let's make our plan of attack for tomorrow," Dad says. "I think we're in for a bumpy ride."

I can't help but think he's right.

When Mom and Dad leave to get their things out of the van I take my binder out. I hear Mr. Harker's voice echo in my head. *"It's fate."*

I never believed in fate, but after he yelled that out I started thinking. I found one of my "friends." Not like I imagined—but still—to actually meet Maybelle Crusher, live and in person; what are the chances?

I sit on a bed and open the binder. I flip through

the pages until I find the picture I drew with the name "Maybelle" scrawled in purple crayon at the top. I'd drawn an arrow from the name to a round girl with long, brown hair. She's holding hands with my cartoon self in a pink house filled with music notes I'd scribbled here and there. There's a unicorn that looks more like a dog with a spike coming out of its forehead, nibbling a flower in the garden surrounding the house.

I turn the pages back toward the front and stop on the picture with the house and the white dog.

My heart aches.

Meeting "Kiki" should've been a "this is the end of your troubles" moment complete with trumpets blaring and angels singing. Instead I can't shake the feeling there's a truckload of crap coming my way. Despite my best efforts to stop it, a tear tumbles down my cheek. Why did Maybelle have to become Kiki and ruin everything?

I wonder how many more of my dreams have to crash and burn before I adopt Mom's robotlike persona.

I slam the binder shut and move the things around in my crate so I can bury it at the bottom. Whatever happens tomorrow, I can't help but think Mr. Harker was right—the die has been cast.

The only question is: at what cost?

6. _Revenge. Hunger. Feed._

My alarm goes off at 5:45 a.m. and I sit up in bed with a start. Whispers tickle my ears and I look wildly around the dark room as the echoes of faint voices fade away. Dark shadows flit and drift around the ceiling with claw-like hands pulling at the air.

Hunger. Feed.

My heart races as I squint, trying to make out the shapes. I turn on the light and see black wisps roll back into themselves until there's nothing.

I rub my eyes and look again. Nothing. Just a dream.

I take a deep calming breath as I sit up. Then I do my

usual "where am I?" and "what do I have to do today" routine to ground myself.

I look around the small room again. South Bristol, Maine. Meet with Kiki. Kill vampires.

I head to the bathroom and look in the mirror and frown. Nothing like bed-head and crease lines from the pillow on my cheek—ugh. Jennifer-Kate has suggested satin pillowcases for better hair and skin in the morning but Mom thought the idea was ridiculous and assumed Jennifer-Kate must have an interest in some pillowcase company.

I splash cold water on my face, run my fingers through my hair and then dig out an assortment of quarters and dollar bills from my purse.

I open my door and head out into the parking lot. A fishy-smelling fog is drifting around in swirls and eddies. I shiver as I head for the soda machine. As I get closer I see someone leaning over to take out a soda.

Tyler Harker.

"Hey," he says and my stomach flips. His eyes are wide and for the first time I notice blue. He stares nervously at me, no doubt because I wasn't too pleasant during our first encounter. He's wearing a tight white shirt and I can't help but notice he's got a better build than I first thought. He should definitely ditch the baggy trench coat. His hair is still hanging in his face, but without the eyeliner he doesn't look half bad.

Too bad he's the enemy. Not to mention a complete jerk.

"Hey," I say nonchalantly, deciding it's best to act a little friendly—keep-your-enemies-close kind of thing. I walk past him and run my fingers through my hair again, wishing I'd brushed it before I'd ventured out and immediately hating myself for thinking that. I smooth the wrinkles on a dollar bill to put in the machine and wait to hear his footsteps walking away.

Nothing.

"No coffee in the rooms—sucks, huh?" he says.

I nod, keeping my attention on the soda machine. "I could tell they wouldn't have free coffee when we pulled in. I've developed a sixth sense for predicting which places have it and which don't. At least there's decent shampoo." The first bill I try is too wrinkled and the machine keeps spitting it out. I take out another and feed it carefully into the slot.

"You're up early," he says.

The bill comes back out toward me and I turn to him with my best evil eye. "Yup, gotta get an early start since we're competing for kills."

I yank out another rejected bill and hear him sigh.

What does he expect? It's bad enough we have to share the job. Does he think I'm going to be all buddy-buddy with him after he and his dad almost stole it from us? Please.

Suddenly he's standing by my side, inserting a crisp bill into the machine. The hairs on the back of my neck rise as his arm briefly bumps up against my shoulder. Goose bumps crop up on his bare, well-toned arm and I wonder if it's from the cold or me. The dollar disappears in the slot and I add two quarters. "Thanks."

I push one of the diet soda buttons and the bottle rattles to the bottom. After I fish it out of the machine, I hand him one of my wrinkled bills but he shakes his head.

"I'm good. It's the least I can do for crashing your territory." His dark bangs fall across his eyes and he brushes them aside. "Look, I know it was a really crappy thing for my dad to do, but he got completely obsessed with coming out here. He's . . ." Tyler looks away. "He's not in a good place, if you know what I mean. He hasn't been for a long time."

Tyler turns away, but I can see that his face registers a mix of embarrassment and sadness. He shakes his head and lets his hair cover his eyes.

I realize my original assessment was wrong. He's not the jerk—I am. I certainly wouldn't want anyone lumping me in the same category as my parents, especially Mom.

"Well, neither of our parents will be getting any awards for child-rearing," I say. "And sorry I kind of bit your head off at the station last night." I look down at the ground and kick at the fog. "It's just that money's tight and my mom was flipping out more than usual." I look back up and notice him watching me through his hair. His light blue irises are rimmed with a darker blue. I realize we're staring at each other and look away while butterflies flit around in my empty stomach.

"Sounds like you could be talking about my dad. Only when money is tight, we sleep in the car."

As if on cue, a car horn blares and we both jump. Kiki is hanging out of the roof of a white limo that's pulling into the parking lot. Her long blond hair is pulled back into a high ponytail and she's wearing a pink hoodie far more modest than the revealing outfit she had on last night. "Daphne," she yells. "Look!" She checks the lot for I don't know what, and then starts laughing maniacally. She pulls out a hunting knife and waves it over her head.

"Whoa," Tyler says. "Who is that?"

I can't help but laugh and give Kiki the thumbs-up. "That would be Kiki Crusher—wannabe vampire slayer."

Tyler looks at me in disbelief as the limo slowly circles the lot with Kiki slashing the air with the knife.

"Long story short, I've been assigned by the South

Bristol vampire task force to give her the 411 on all things undead."

"She's going to hurt someone with that knife," he says, watching Kiki stab at the fog.

"That's kind of the point" I giggle. "Pun intended. But you know after you stake 'em — off comes the head."

He turns back to me. "Huh? Why would you do that?"

I raise my eyebrows in surprise. "You *don't*?"

His gets a stupid smirk on face. It reminds me of his father, and my annoyance returns.

"No, I don't," he says, looking at me like I'm the crazy one. "But given what my dad said about your parents I'm not surprised they have you beheading *dead* vampires." His smile broadens. "You either stake them or cut the head off — one or the other, babe."

Babe? I put a hand on one hip. "My *name* is Daphne. And your father's far from perfect. I heard his demon theory — that's a little out there, don't you think?"

Tyler stiffens. "Maybe it is and maybe it isn't." He folds his arms across his chest. "But at least he's not having me follow antiquated slayer practices that have no basis in reality."

"At least my father never had to . . ." My mouth opens and my stomach drops. I can hardly believe what was about to come out of my mouth.

He stares at me—his jaw locked and his angry blue eyes dare me to finish the sentence. I feel sick and wish I could rewind time and take it all back.

I swallow hard. "Uh, I don't have time for this," I say trying to sound all businesslike and not at all like I was about to bring up what happened to his mother. "I have work to do."

Kiki skips up to us and eyes Tyler. "Hellooooo," she says, taking him in.

"Hey," he says, totally staring at her chest.

I retract my earlier thought about her modest attire. Kiki's hoodie is unzipped just enough to reveal a black lace cami her boobs are in danger of spilling out of. She's wearing black leggings that show off every curve. The whole ensemble's pretty hoochie for hunting vampires. At least she's got on a pair of pink high-tops instead of heels.

I can't help but notice that even though she's obviously made an effort to dress down, she still took the time to put on a ton of makeup. She elbows my side and gives me a look that says she wants an introduction. "Sooooo, who's your new *friend*?" she asks drawing out the words.

I scoff. "He's not my friend; he's just some guy who horned in on our gig."

Tyler shakes his head in disgust. "Guess what—any handshake agreement our parents had is officially null and void. If you want the job, make sure you do a better job than us." He gives Kiki a brusque nod. "Nice meeting you."

"I'm Kiki!" she calls out as he marches toward his room. "Hopefully I'll see you again soon!"

"Tyler," he says without turning around.

She tilts her head and watches him walk away. When he slams his door shut, she turns to me. "Are you always so rude to hot guys?"

"He's not hot, he's just another slayer. He and his dad had an agreement with my parents not to get jobs in the same area, but here they are nonetheless."

"Mmmm. Maybe I can work with *him* next time." She wiggles her eyebrows up and down. "I'd let him slay me anytime!"

I scowl at her and rub my arms to chase away the chill. I glance at his room. "Do you really think he's hot?"

"I could stare into those baby-blues twenty-four-seven. Did you notice the darker blue on the outside of his irises?"

"I guess." I fold my arms across my chest. Apparently my boobs were nothing to openly gawk at. "He's a jerk."

"So is Gabe, but he's still good in the—"

"Tyler wears a black trench coat and eyeliner," I interrupt. Kiki is obviously the kind of girl who tells her friends *everything*, and I don't think I could stomach listening to her bedroom antics—not when I've never even held hands with a guy or gotten one to stare at my chest.

"Ew. Guy-liner?" Kiki wrinkles her nose and snaps her fingers dismissively in the air. "Dealbreaker. I'm more partial to blonds anyway."

I smile. The last thing I need is a budding romance between Kiki and Tyler. I tilt my head toward my room. "Let me get my stuff and we can get started." We start walking and I feel drained from my encounter with Tyler. Talk about an energy vampire—someone needs to put a psychic stake through him and his father.

Kiki bounces along beside me. "I'm so excited!" she gushes, grinning. "I woke up at five and couldn't go back to sleep."

"You're awfully perky for having gotten up at five o'clock in the morning. Shouldn't you be hung over or something?"

"Going to the police station seriously cut down on my drinking last night—do you know how many papers we had to sign? It was ridiculous. All they need is one form that says 'tell no one or we ship you off to Area 51'!"

I laugh. "Yeah, dealing with vampires seems to require a ton of paperwork."

"Anyway, I've had at least four cups of coffee this

morning. I wanted to be ready for action!" She does a few karate chops in the air and then a roundhouse kick. At least she manages to stay upright this time.

I slide my key card in the door and lead Kiki in. She looks around the little room with the tacky bedspreads and I can't help but feel self-conscious. "Home sweet home," I say, trying to sound lighthearted. "When you're a full-fledged slayer like me you, too, can live in the lap of luxury."

She plops herself on the unused bed. "So slaying doesn't pay too much?"

I pull a brush through my hair and start to braid it. "Nope. The big bucks go to paying off witnesses—I just do it because I love working with vampires." I give her a look so she'll know I'm kidding. "We do get full government health insurance; that's supposed to make up for the low pay, but we're kind of at the mercy of town budgets. A lot of slayers have full- or part-time jobs on the side. Lucky me—my parents decided to make a career out of it."

"What about big cities? They must pay better."

The cities do pay better, and over the years I've repeatedly asked my parents to put in for a metro-gig so we could stay in one place and I could have some semblance of a life. But they always said it's the little towns that need the most help. It's embarrassing to admit my parents chose the "little towns" over me. "Most of the big cities have in-house hunters. We're freelancers," I say, hoping she won't ask more and we can move on.

"How often do you get to go home?"

I turn away from her and rifle through my toiletry bag. "We don't."

"So your house is just sitting empty all the time or do you have relatives living in it?"

I take in a deep breath, turn back to her and force a smile on my face. I wave around the room. "This is home. And we used to travel with my grandfather until he was institution-alized. He passed away ten years ago. I don't think my mom has any family left—at least she's never talked about them."

"Oh," Kiki says quietly. "I guess if you're always trav-eling around a lot it doesn't make sense to have a house."

"Exactly." Tears prick my eyes and I turn from her and blink them away. "So, how about we start today's lesson."

"Wait," Kiki says. She opens her large pink bag and takes out a handheld recorder and a spiral notebook. She turns the recorder on and holds it toward me. "What do I need to know?"

I point to the recorder. "Is that necessary?"

"I don't want to miss anything."

"No recordings."

"Fine," she says, putting it away.

"Okay, you know the basics — stake in the heart." I put my hand over my heart. "I don't know if you know this, but it's located a little to the left of—"

"Got it covered," she says. She rifles through her bag and pulls out a folder. She opens it and takes out a diagram showing a heart inside a rib cage. "I did some research last night. I also found this cool website that sells vampire stakes. Look at these." She takes out some more printouts and spreads them on the bed. "I ordered a few of these and a couple of these," she says, pointing to some intricately carved stakes. "I wasn't sure which ones would be the most durable; we'll have to test them out."

I look at the stakes and roll my eyes. "These may be pretty, but if they break, you're screwed."

"Well, it would be way more convenient if you could use, say, a metal stake that wouldn't break. Can we?"

"The theory is they have to be staked by something that was once alive."

"Is that the same kind of theory that thinks it's a necessity to decapitate heads after you stake the body?"

I toss her a stake. "Just use this. Trust me; it'll get the job done."

She grimaces as she catches it. "It looks like a fence post."

"I *know*, you already mentioned that," I say, finding

it difficult to hide my annoyance. "But they're cheap and they work."

She puts the stake down on the bed, folds her hands in her lap, and looks at me like I'm a small child who doesn't know the first thing about hunting. "Daphne, just because the cheap prototype stake works doesn't mean you should ignore the kick-ass, hand-turned, spindle-style, aged-cedar stake with leather covered handle for a 'sure grip.'"

She holds up a picture and I have to admit it does look cool. Of course owning something like that sends the message that you enjoy hunting vampires. Which I do not.

She picks up another picture. "And look at this one — cherry-stained hawthorn with *roses* carved on it. Is that totally sweet or what?"

I look at the price and almost faint. "It's also two hundred dollars — that's almost half of what we're getting paid per kill. And I'm fairly certain the people making these are not expecting them to be plunged into any actual vampires."

She pouts. "But they're so pretty."

"If you want to use the fancy stakes I won't stop you."

She bounces on the bed. "Yay! I'm having them express-mailed so they should arrive tomorrow. I was even toying with the idea of having one specially made." She grins. "How *awesome* would it be to have a stake carved like a *unicorn's horn*? Every time I plunged it into a vampire's heart it'd be like—*take that, Mom and Dad. I don't need your stinking television show!*"

I stare at her. "Wow. That's just . . . disturbing."

She puts her hands up and nods. "Okay, maybe that's going a little too far. I guess I have some unresolved issues with my parents."

"Yeah. In the meantime, do you think you could stomach using one of the *boring* stakes?"

She picks one up and pumps her arm up and down like she's plunging it into someone's chest. "It's a little heavy, and a rounded handle would be a little more ergonomic, but I guess I can make do."

"Glad to hear it."

She opens her notebook and takes out a pen. It looks like she has a bunch of notes under the heading "Vampires" written in purple ink. "So about sunlight—scorching end to vampires—true or false?"

"False. A vampire's powers are greatly diminished during the daytime hours, though. That's why we house-clean during the day and go street hunting at night when they're more likely to be trolling for victims."

She makes some notes and then looks up at me. "Silver bullets good for vampires as well as werewolves?"

"Only werewolves—but they're a dying breed and not

worth worrying about. Nowadays lycanthropy is easy to keep under control with drugs during the time of change so their population is declining rapidly."

She bites on the pen cap. "So you're telling me I'm not going to get any hot wolf action from the alpha male who battled his pack to win me as his mate?"

I laugh. "Sorry."

She clucks her tongue and crosses out something in her notebook with bold strokes. "Okay, what's the scoop on garlic?"

"They don't like the smell and stuffing it in the mouth of a decapitated head helps prevent it from . . ." I pause when I see her rolling her eyes.

"Really? The undead are that bothered by garlic? Even the decapitated heads?"

"Tradition says they are. And you said you'd cut the heads off—that's the only reason I agreed to work with you."

"I thought it had to with the money," she shoots back. "But you're the boss." She puts her pen to paper. "Put garlic in the mouth of *severed* head so vampire with *stake* in its *heart* won't *somehow* magically reattach it." She marks the sentence with an exclamation point and then looks up at me innocently. "Can they really turn into bats?"

"I've been told it's possible for them to shape-shift but

I've never seen it happen. It could be only the really old ones can do it."

She smirks. "So you're admitting you don't know everything about vampires?"

"Kiki, we're cutting the heads off."

"Yeah, yeah. What's next?"

"For this job we had to split the houses to be cleaned with the Harkers—that's that Tyler guy you met in the parking lot and his whack-job father. The police divvied up the houses believed to have vampires in them and we each have our own lists. There's been a large migration of vampires into the area recently, so at night we'll patrol the downtown area for vamps looking for dinner and preying upon the kindness of strangers in hopes of getting invited into a home."

"So they have to be invited in?"

"Yup."

"Must be invited in," she says as she writes it down.

"These roaming vamps are up for grabs, and any one you kill counts for Team Van Helsing."

"Wait, if I kill one, why don't *I* get to keep the money?"

"Because you're my apprentice."

"Fine, it's not like I need it anyway."

"Must be nice," I say under my breath. I drag a duffel bag out of the closet and heft it on to my bed. "Let's load up." I unzip it and reveal my supply of stakes and garlic. "We have a skeleton key that will open just about any lock, but we have to be careful once we enter a house because there's no telling where the vampire might be resting—or waiting. You need to be on high alert. New vampires are a little blood-crazed and since the vampire phenomena in town is recent, it's likely there will be a lot of newbies. On the plus side, ninety percent of the time they're zonked out during the day and you can just walk in and stake them before they even know what's going on."

"What about the other ten percent of the time?"

"They jump out and scare the crap out of you and *then* you stake them."

She wrinkles her nose. "I don't like things jumping out at me."

"No one does. The other thing you need to know is you have to apply *a lot* of pressure to get the stake to penetrate the rib cage. It's a lot harder than it looks and you really have to put some muscle in it and puncture the heart."

She sits up straight with a look of resolve on her face. "Will do!"

I look around the room. "I wish we had something you could practice on. My parents used to have me train on watermelons. I guess it doesn't matter since I'll be doing all the staking today anyway."

She gives me a pouty look. "Fine," I say, "if we come across a really easy job I'll let you have a crack at it."

She pumps a fist in the air. "Yay!"

My lip curls up in disgust. She's way too cheery about the whole thing. I push up a pant leg and strap on my knife and sheath.

Her eyes widen as she watches me. "Ooooh—I need one of those. It's very assassin-chic. I'll have to look for something like that online."

I want to tell her not to bother since she'll probably quit after the first house, but I keep my mouth shut. "Let me call my parents to let them know we're heading out. They'll hunt together and we'll check in after each house cleaning. Are you ready?"

She grins crazily. "This is going to be so awesome!"

7.

"I was thinking we could go back to my place afterward," Kiki says as we trek down the dirt road in the woods. "I found some great pants that I think would be good for hunting and want your opinion. They're kind of a yoga-pants style for freedom of movement but made of tougher material."

"Hey, there it is, through the trees." I point to a log cabin–styled vacation home. It's perched on a small piece of land jutting out into the Damariscotta River. Fog is rolling across the surface of the water buoyed along by the cool breeze that carries the smell of pine and salt water.

When I was little I used to ask my parents if we could

stop at a Christmas tree stand every December just so I could walk around and smell the pines. I would "pick out" which tree I wanted and imagine bringing home and decorating it. One year Dad bought a small, plastic tree with blinking lights for our hotel room and couldn't understand why I was disappointed.

I turn to Kiki and realize she's staring at the cabin like it's a ghost.

"Come on, let's get our stakes out." I unzip my bag and take out a stake while we make our way across a short wooden bridge traversing a tidal stream.

Kiki nods and pulls one out of her purse, but doesn't say anything.

I stumble on a root and she reaches out a hand to steady me.

"Thanks." I smile, but she doesn't notice — her eyes are fixed on our goal.

"Maybe we should've brought my bodyguard," she says quietly.

It's a pretty bumpy road, with rocks and tree roots exposed from spring washouts. Sam offered to come with us when he determined the limo couldn't negotiate the road, but Kiki insisted we could handle it ourselves.

After I assured him the risk during the daytime was extremely low, it didn't take much to convince him to stay put. As tough as Sam is, I'm guessing that he's had his fill of vampires.

Traveling by limo is something I could totally get used to, though. We had the most amazing hot, toffee-flavored coffee, with pastries and fresh-squeezed juice set out for us on a little table. Kiki kept the music on shuffle and told me the names of each of the bands, and I thoroughly enjoyed the break from the all-news stations my parents like to listen to. We kept the skylight open even though it's still chilly, and I felt like a movie star instead of the loser slayer that I am.

I glance at Kiki. It's weird having her so quiet—so un-Kiki-like. She was very chatty on the ride over. She told me stories about working on The Disco Unicorn set and how one time she defiled a whole carton of Sugar LeBlanc action figures by drawing nipples and pubic hair on the naked dolls. She then redressed them and they were then given out at a charity concert. We'd both laughed as she mimicked the PR guy running around like a chicken with his head cut off trying to calm the angry parents and write a plausible press release that wouldn't tarnish the Disco Unicorn's reputation.

Now she's walking slowly with grim determination; her mouth is pinched and her nostrils are flaring. I imagine the reality—and sheer foolishness—of voluntarily going after vampires has started to sink in.

"You don't have to do this," I tell her.

She licks her lips—her eyes still locked on the cabin. "I'm good," she says in a voice an octave higher than normal.

She's looking a little pale, and it's tempting to tease her, but I decide to give her a break. Even though I've done this hundreds of times, the adrenaline is already coursing through my system and I had to choke down a few ant-acids before we got out of the limo. Even in the daylight, walking into a dark house knowing there's something that would love to rip your throat out is more than a little dis-concerting.

It's actually kind of comforting having Kiki here. I used to hunt with Mom most of the time, but over the last year I've been going solo more often than not. Mom has a habit of running some incomprehensible dialog just under her breath whenever we're casing out a house. She sounds like a crazy person and it makes it hard to focus.

We approach the cabin and I take it in. Each window is shuttered with plywood—probably done when the own-ers closed it up for the season—making for a cozy retreat for the undead. It's fairly small, so hopefully it won't take too long to flush out our vamp.

The front-door knob and lock have been ripped off, and I point to them lying in the pine needles to the right of the steps. "That's what usually tips the police off," I say quietly. "If they know vampires are in the area they keep watch over empty houses like this for signs of entry."

"I thought a vampire had to be invited in," she whispers.

"It's an empty house that isn't a primary residence, so it's fair game."

Kiki's eyes pop. "I'm staying at our vacation cottage. What if I come home and there's a vampire in the hot tub?"

I almost laugh imagining a Speedo-clad vampire lounging in a hot tub sipping a literal Bloody Mary. "Do you consider your vacation house *home*?"

She purses her lips and nods. "It's way homier than our place in Beverly Hills. I spend most of my time here anyways."

"Then you're good. A vampire would definitely have to be invited in."

She visibly relaxes until I put a finger to my lips and tilt my head toward the door. She takes a deep breath and I see the hand holding her stake is shaking.

"Since we don't need to use a key, I'm going to quietly push the door open. I don't think we'll have any problems, but follow closely behind and be prepared for *anything*. Do you have your flashlight?"

She nods ever so slightly, and takes a flashlight out of

her bag. There's a greenish tinge to her skin and she looks like she's about to throw up.

"If we're lucky, the vampire will be in a deep sleeplike state and we can be back in the limo in no time," I say reassuringly.

One corner of her mouth twitches like she's trying to smile. I give her the thumbs-up, but figure Kiki Crusher's vampire-slaying gig will be short-lived.

I take out a small but powerful flashlight and hold it in my left hand while I grip my stake with my right. I lean into the door and push on it gently with my shoulder. It creaks open and Kiki grimaces at the noise.

I step in the entryway, shining the light and illuminating sheet-covered furniture and a small kitchenette. Large, rough beams flank the two-story ceiling, giving the otherwise small cabin a cavernous feel. There's only one main room with the kitchen and sitting area sharing the open floor plan. A staircase leads to an open loft I assume is the bedroom. There doesn't appear to be a basement, which is fine by me. If I had to pick a house to clean with a wannabe slayer this would be the one, because there aren't too many places to hide.

I wave behind my back and gesture for Kiki to follow. She comes in and glues herself to my side. I can feel her heart thudding against my shoulder.

"Anything?" she whispers breathlessly in my ear.

I shake my head and shine the light along the wall and see two closed doors—probably a bathroom and a closet. I take a few steps toward the doors and the sound echoes around us.

"I'm going to open the first door," I whisper.

She nods.

I carefully make my way to the door, put my hand on the knob, and listen for any noise. I throw the door open, flashing the light inside and see it's the bathroom with a dark curtain drawn across a tub—great. My heart pounds in my chest and I can hear my blood pumping fast in my ears. I can't count the number of times we've found vamps lurking in the tub. It does make it easier to clean up the blood, but you never know if they're lying in it or just waiting behind the curtain to get you.

I tread lightly over the tiles toward the tub—lavender-scented soap permeates the air and stings my nose. I take slow deep breaths to calm my heart, raise my stake, and pull back the curtain, poised to strike.

It's empty.

"All clear," I say in a hushed voice. I turn and Kiki isn't behind me. My stomach feels like it's been dropped fifty feet down a mine shaft. "Kiki?" I whisper desperately.

I rush out of the bathroom and see she's standing just to

the side of the door sweeping her flashlight back and forth across the room. I exhale. "Oh, thank God! I thought . . ." It suddenly occurs to me how stupid this arrangement is. At the very least she should be with Mom and Dad so one of them could keep an eye on her. If something happens to her I don't know if I'll be able to forgive myself.

"I was making sure nothing snuck up on you," she says.

I shine the light at her and she blinks and shields her eyes. She looks a little calmer now and she actually smiles at me.

"Good thinking. Um, I'll get the next door." I turn around and go through the same routine, but it's only a closet with a mop and broom and a few lightweight coats and rubber boots.

"Loft?" Kiki suggests.

"Stay down here." I do one more sweep with my flashlight to make sure I haven't missed anything. I direct the beam on the couches but it doesn't appear anything is hiding under the sheets.

I point the light up the stairs and start up. Each creaky board gets my pulse racing again. It'll be my head that pops up into the loft first and I've seen enough horror movies to know this is not a good thing. Picturing something cutting my head off and having it fall down the stairs and land at Kiki's feet is not helping my nerves.

I pause just before I enter the loft and then race up the last few steps, stake ready. There's a king-size platform bed stripped down to the bare mattress, two nightstands and a dresser against the far wall. I slowly walk to the other side of the bed but my guard is already down. There may have been a vampire here earlier, but it appears it's moved on.

I walk to the rail and lean over and shine my flashlight at Kiki. "I hate to disappoint you, but this place is already clean."

She laughs with relief. "Will it affect my street cred as a slayer if I admit I'm *totally* okay with that?"

"I won't say a word."

She lets out a long breath as she plops down on one of the covered couches and drops her stake on the coffee table with a clank. "Is it also okay to admit I thought I was going to pee in my pants? I don't know how the hell you do this." She turns her flashlight on and off waving it around the room like a strobe light. "You made it look so easy in the alley, but actually going into a home and opening closed doors . . ." She visibly shivers. "This is crazy shit."

Bingo. "Are you trying to tell me you want to give up vampire hunting?"

"I don't know. After seeing what that vampire was

doing to Sam—what it could've done to me—and then having you out of the blue save us, well, I thought I'd found my calling. I've had so many 'callings' since I quit the band, and none of them have panned out. My therapist says I lost my way after my parents replaced me on their TV show. But after I stopped being a backup dancer I tried . . ." Suddenly Kiki stops turning the light on and off and focuses the beam above my head. Her eyes widen. "Daphne—on the ceiling . . ."

A wave of icy terror slaps me as I look up and see a man somehow defying gravity as he scurries across the ceiling toward me like a spider. He leaps down and lands catlike on the rafter above me. His eyes are black as tar and he smiles, revealing two impossibly large canine teeth. Before I can even fully register what I'm seeing, he jumps down to the loft and knocks me onto the bed like a rag doll. I lose my grip on the stake and hear it clatter to the floor.

I try to roll off the bed, but he pins me with one arm and tears away at my shirt with sharp fingernails. He grabs my braid and pulls my head back and stares down at me hungrily. He licks his lips and then plunges at my chest—classic I-don't-want-it-to-get-noticed spot. I gasp as his teeth sink into my flesh above my breast—but then a calmness flows through me. The pain disappears. I hear him sucking hungrily and feel like I'm floating. Warmth radiates from his bite. Electric shocks tingle under the trail of his hand at it roams my body. I lean my hips into him and I want to beg him to never stop, but I can't find my voice.

"Get off her, you freaking psycho!"

Suddenly his mouth is torn from me and I cry out. "No!" Pain radiates from my wounds and I push myself up and try to clear my head.

Kiki is stabbing the vampire in the back with her hunting knife. He howls in frustration, my blood spraying from his mouth. He turns and pulls the knife from Kiki's hand and throws it over the loft rail into the main room. She screams as he grabs her by her ponytail and drags her to the rail, pinning her with his body.

I can't let anything happen to her.

My body still feels fuzzy and I struggle to get my knife from its sheath on my leg. With every ounce of energy I can muster, I raise my arm and come down hard on the back of his neck. Bones crack and I'm sure I've partially severed his spinal cord. This distracts him enough for Kiki to push him back. He lands on the bed and she's on him. Stake raised high, she plunges it directly into his heart on the first try. He goes limp and I swipe my blade, hacking against his neck until it's severed all the way through.

Kiki and I stare down at him—our labored breathing the only sound.

"I thought you said they aren't very powerful in the daytime," she manages to say in between gasping breaths.

"They're not supposed to be. I've never seen anything like this before. It was like he was at full power times ten." The body hasn't decayed much so he's not one of the ancient vampires that are stronger than normal. What gives?

"You didn't tell me they were wall-crawlers like Spider-Man either."

I look at her helplessly. "I've never seen one do that." I cover my mouth with my hand and force myself to take slower breaths through my nose. What the hell kind of vampire was he?

"You're bleeding."

I look down at my chest and besides the puncture wounds there are deep scratches from where he ripped at my shirt.

"Let me get something to stop it." She runs down the stairs and I hear her ripping a sheet. I collapse on the bed next to the vampire trying to understand what just happened.

She pounds back up, and I take the ripped piece from her. I wince as I put pressure on my wounds. "Well, we're even now. I saved your life and you saved mine."

"Wow. I did, didn't I?" She sits next to me. "Holy unicorn shit. I just killed my first vampire." She gives a little laugh. "When you opened that bathroom door I wanted to run the hell out of this place and curl up in a ball and cry—but now I am officially *Kiki Crusher, vampire slayer*."

We both do jazz hands and despite the pain, I laugh. I imagine we look surreal—two girls—one half-dressed and bleeding—giggling on a bed next to a decapitated vampire with a stake in his chest.

"If this were a fairy tale your debt to me would be paid and we could each ride off into our own sunset," I offer.

She shakes her head. "I'm not going anywhere. I know people in this town. What if they get Dorothy who runs the bookstore—or Gabe—or even Shelly who is always trying to stop me from ordering more drinks?"

I look her in the eye. "Are you *really* up for another house cleaning?"

"Are you?"

"I guess so. My mother would certainly expect me to be." I look over at the vampire. "It's never been this bad during the daytime; I think this guy was some sort of fluke. I'm also thinking I'll need a couple of painkillers before the next house. If you want to call it quits though, I *totally* understand."

She sniffs. "I'm not going to let you do it by yourself—you almost got killed just now."

I want to protest, but she's right. I was sloppy. In my defense I've never seen a vampire crawling around on the ceiling before, but still . . .

"Why do your parents let you hunt alone? Aren't they worried you might . . . you know . . ."

Her question makes my stomach churn uncomfortably. I've asked myself this question before. How can two people be hell-bent on protecting others but put their child in harm's way? "I don't know," I say, not wanting to admit that hunting vampires is an obsession with my parents—one that supersedes me.

She picks up my torn shirt—it looks like someone slashed it with a knife. "This is trashed. Take this." Kiki unzips her hoodie and hands it to me.

"Thanks." I remove the sheet from my chest and see most of the bleeding has stopped. The long scratch marks throb and I grimace in pain when I reach out and take the hoodie. It's warm and smells like perfume—something I've never had.

I put it on and realize this is as close as I'll ever get to sharing clothes with a friend. In a *Jennifer-Kate* piece, she cautioned readers to make sure each article of borrowed clothing gets returned in good shape. I've already gotten blood on the inside of the hoodie, but I know Kiki won't mind.

Jennifer-Kate knows everything about fashion but shit about vampires.

"Did it hurt?" Kiki asks as I zip the hoodie up. "You know—the vampire. I asked Sam about it, but he'd only say it was something he'd like to forget."

While I doubt Kiki has any interest in dating a vampire now, I decide not to tell her how frighteningly good it felt. Now I understand what the vampire-fetish groupies find appealing about the whole thing. I'm pretty sure my particular vampire wasn't in it for a quick fix—he seemed like he was going to go all the way and I would've ended up like Mrs. Harker.

"Let's just say it sucked," I finally say. "And I can't believe I got groped by a vampire. Not what I was expecting for the first time someone touched my boobs."

"You've *never* been felt up before? Ever?" She stares at me like this is crazier than killing vampires.

"I've never even held hands with a guy! I drive around the country in a van with my parents. How exactly am I going to meet someone and get to know him well enough so I'd *want* him to feel my boobs?"

My fantasy prom date, Brad, flashes into my head.

If only.

Kiki shakes her head. "Daphne, Daphne, Daphne. That is what a one-night stand is for—or what I have with Gabe. You don't necessarily need to know them well or even like them for a good booty call."

I know what Jennifer-Kate would say to that, but since Kiki and I are getting along at the moment I decide not to mention it. "I couldn't do that. I think you need time to get to know someone—build up trust."

She smirks. "You might be surprised how quickly you can *build trust* with the right person, but you do what feels right and I'll do what feels *good*."

I roll my eyes. "Let me call the kill in and we can hit our next house."

Kiki jumps up and pumps a fist in the air. "I'm ready. Let's kick some more ass for team Van Helsing!"

I smile comes to my lips. Kiki isn't going away anytime soon—and I'm glad.

8.

We leave the second house, a ritzy vacation chalet, a little worse for the wear.

"How about we call it a day?" I suggest even though it's only eleven o'clock. My entire body aches. I have never taken a beating like this before. I check my phone — still no reply from Mom and Dad. They always check in. Worry runs through me like cold water.

Kiki nods. "Three on two," she says as we slowly make our way to the limo. "Holy shit, that was crazy, and that one was like a *kid*—maybe eleven or twelve."

"He looked like a kid but he was *old*. Did you see the rate of decomposition after you staked him? There wasn't much left besides bone and dried connective tissue."

She shudders. "That was so fucked-up."

"Yeah." That little "kid" threw me into a wall with the force of a Mack truck.

The front of the hoodie Kiki lent me is soaked in blood, and one of the straps of her cami has been torn off. Our pants are ripped at the knees, and we're battered, bruised, and bloody.

Kiki leans over and puts her hands on her thighs and inhales deeply. She tilts her head up at me. "Are you *sure* they're supposed be weaker during the daytime? Are you sure you didn't get that backward?"

Before I can answer Sam jumps out of the limo and gasps when he sees us. He's probably six foot five and three hundred pounds of muscle and I'm thinking Kiki should have tried a little harder to get him to fight with us.

"Miss Crusher, your parents would kill me if they knew I was allowing this."

She holds a hand up to his face. "We talked about this last night. I *need* to do this so don't even *think* of telling my parents I'm hunting vampires."

"But surely—"

Kiki points at him. "I'm a big girl; I can take care of myself!"

He nods. "How many this time?"

Kiki holds up three fingers. "And I got the worst one!"

Despite his objections to the hunt, I can't help but think he looks a little proud. He opens the door to the back and Kiki drags herself in. Sam puts an arm out and blocks me from going in. He gives me a look like it's my fault Kiki is risking her life. "If anything happens to her . . ."

"This was her idea." I gesture toward Kiki. "And do you ever have much success getting her to take 'no' for an answer?"

His eyes soften and he shakes his head.

"But I'll do everything I can to make sure nothing happens to her." As I join Kiki in the back, all I can think is what might have happened to me if she wasn't there. The vampires in South Bristol are on crack or something.

Kiki groans and closes her eyes as Sam pulls the limo away from the curb. "We need a drink."

"It's not even noon and you promised you wouldn't drink on the job. Besides, I have to go out again tonight for street patrol."

She sticks her tongue out. "Yes, Mom." She opens one eye and looks at me. "I'm guessing you've never even been drunk before."

I fold my arms across my chest. "Like that's a bad thing?"

She sits up and rolls her eyes. "I know you've led a somewhat *strange* and sheltered life, but your bucket list now includes getting felt up by a guy with a pulse and getting drunk. You don't have to get puking drunk or anything, but God, you need to live a little."

"I drank a whole beer once even though my parents have told me—"

"Hey," she interrupts, hitting me on the shoulder.

"Ow, what was that for?"

"Look, it's your friend." She leans forward and knocks on the partition. "Sam! Pull over by that guy in the unfortunate trench coat."

Tyler Harker is talking on his cell phone by the side of the road. "He's not my friend," I insist. "Keep going, Sam."

"Don't listen to her, pull over," Kiki insists. She lowers her window. "Hey, Slayer-dude, do you need a ride?"

Tyler is completely taken aback and briefly glances over his shoulder as if Kiki is addressing some other vampire slayer nearby. "Me?"

"Yes, you—we met this morning in the parking lot, remember?"

"Kiki," I say through clenched teeth. *"What are you doing?"*

She turns to me, grabs her breasts with both hands, and then points to Tyler.

My face flushes. "Oh, my God, are you kidding me? *Not going to happen!*"

"I'd bet he'd be happy to feel you up; a guy like that has probably never even touched a boob," she hurriedly whispers to me. She sticks her head out the window again. "So Daphne and I just cleaned a couple of houses, *if you know what I mean*, and I was thinking we might want to hit the hot tub at my house to unwind a bit. Care to join us?"

I lean my head back and whimper.

"Um, no, thanks. I'm going to go back to my hotel room; I just talked to my dad and he's on his way to pick me up."

Kiki scoffs. "You're turning down a limo ride and a *hot tub* so you can hang with your *dad*? Are you kidding me? Oh, and we have freshly brewed *coffee*," she sings. "Really good coffee."

He raises his eyebrows and I glare at Kiki. I had told her earlier how our crappy hotel didn't even have free coffee and how heavenly it was to get some of the good stuff.

He brushes the hair out of his eyes and looks at us uncomfortably. "Um, my dad wants to work on this theory he has and I kind of have to help. He'll get really pissed if I blow it off."

"Well, we can drive you to the hotel and compare notes," she continues. "You won't believe the shit these vamps put us through today. Right, Daphne?"

She pulls me over to the window and I nod wearily.

"I won't take 'no' for an answer. After all, we slayers have to stick together."

He looks past Kiki—his blue eyes lock onto mine. "Not *everyone* shares that sentiment."

My stomach flutters and I wish he'd look away. "That's because *everyone* has their own way of doing things, and just because someone does something the other someone doesn't, doesn't mean they shouldn't be doing it or should be made fun of!"

Kiki raises an eyebrow. "Okay, Daphne, I have no idea what the hell you just said." She turns to Tyler who is rolling his eyes. "Have I missed something?"

"No!" I say before he can respond. "But my parents don't want me hanging around with him."

"Oh, for God's sake, what are you, two?" Kiki chides. "Who cares what your parents say?" She sticks her arm out and motions toward Tyler's phone. "Call your father," she commands.

Tyler nods. "Okay." He opens his phone and pushes a button. "Uh, Dad," he says after a few seconds. "I don't need a ride." He turns his back to us. "I'll be right there—I just have to do something. Just something, okay? I know, I'll be there."

He listens for a few more seconds and then shuts the

phone. Kiki opens the door, and as he approaches, grabs the sleeve of his coat and pulls him to the limo. He takes the seat opposite me and she shuts the door. "Sam, could you take us to the hotel?"

"Yes, Miss Crusher."

"Thanks, big guy."

Tyler looks around the limo appreciatively. He's dressed in head-to-toe black again, and the guy-liner is back. He's wearing some sort of cologne that pleasantly reminds me of ginger snaps. He rubs his hands over the soft leather seats. "Not bad."

"It's the *only* way to hunt vampires," Kiki says. She points to the large thermos of coffee as the limo pulls away from the curb. "Interested?"

"Thanks, that'd be . . ." His eyes widen as he finally takes a good look at us. "Whoa, what happened to you two?"

My face flushes as I remember it looks like I've been through a wood chipper. I peek at my reflection in the tinted window. Half of my hair has come unbraided and is sticking out at odd angles, I have a red welt across one cheek, and the bite marks on my chest are visible. I quickly zip the bloody hoodie all the way.

Kiki gapes at him. "I think the real question is what *didn't* happen to you? Do you see him, Daphne? Not a scratch!" She gives Tyler a once-over and then draws her lips back in an exaggerated grimace. "Oooooh," she says drawing out the word. "I'm sorry. You struck out." She sits up proudly and smirks at me. "Looks like Team Van Helsing is *kicking your butt*. We already dispatched four vampires."

She raises a palm in my direction and I reluctantly high-five her.

His lips turn up into a smug smile. "Actually, I cleaned all five houses on my list for a total of six vampires."

Kiki's mouth drops open. "Are you shitting us?"

I stare at him in disbelief. "Six? Already?"

He leans back into the seat, flashing a cocky smile. "You can check with the vampire task-force agents if you don't believe me."

Kiki looks back and forth between Tyler and me. "Okay, you seriously need to tell us what we're doing wrong because we got our asses handed to us today."

"We got *four*! That's only two less than he did."

"But look at us," she shoots back. "And you got bitten!"

My face flushes even deeper. "Didn't have to mention that," I say through the corner of my mouth.

I see him eyeing my neck for signs of a bite and I'm glad the vamp got me in the chest so the telltale marks aren't so visible. He shifts uncomfortably and looks away.

"So what are you doing that we aren't?" Kiki asks.

He tilts his head so his bangs hang down and cover his eyes. "I, uh, really don't like to talk about it, okay?"

"Come on," Kiki says. "Don't be all 'super secret slayer' on us. We need help."

"No, we *don't*."

She holds out her hands in front of my face. "I broke *six* nails today, Daphne. With this crazy schedule you have me on, when I am supposed to go to the salon?" She turns to Tyler. "Details, please!"

Tyler has a pained expression on his face like he'd rather get his butt kicked by a vampire than tell us anything. "I can't. It's beyond embarrassing," he says quietly. "And *really* twisted."

Kiki leans in toward him. "You don't know 'embarrassing' and 'twisted' until you've danced backup in a thirty pound unicorn costume while singing songs about *fruit* and *puppies*."

He stares at her.

"Long story," she says, leaning back. "Anyway . . . who better to understand than us? Right, Daphne?"

I nod. I have to admit I'm curious. I mean, there isn't a scratch on him.

He straightens his trench coat and purses his lips.

"We're here for you," she coos. "And if I knew some

surefire way to kill vampires without getting the WWE treatment, I would tell *you*."

He gives me a sullen look.

"So would I," I say begrudgingly. "This is kill or be killed, after all."

He lets out a long breath. "Okay." He taps his foot a few times on the floor. "You know how there's people who, you know, let vampires feed on them?"

Kiki and I exchange looks and I know we're both wondering where he's going with this.

"Yeah," we respond in unison.

"Well, some of those people have formed a group, The Ankh Society, and they have a certain look and way of dressing that tells a vampire you'll let them feed."

Kiki grimaces. "After what I've seen today I can't believe anyone would *let* them do that. What's in it for the Ankh weirdos?"

"It's supposed to feel *really* good," he says without enthusiasm. "Really, really good."

Kiki's mouth opens and she points a finger in my face. "You lied to me!"

I hold my hands out as I feel my cheeks turn to crimson. The last thing I wanted was for Kiki or Tyler Harker to know I got off on a vampire bite.

"I said getting bitten 'sucked.' I just didn't tell you I

was being *literal*. And it was for your own protection, what with you and your obsession with getting a supernatural *booty call*," I insist.

Tyler appraises us with a bemused smile.

"It's not funny!" I snap.

His smile disappears and he shakes his head. "Sorry, I've just never heard the term 'supernatural booty call' before."

Kiki giggles and I can't stop the corners of my mouth from turning up. "She thought she wanted a vampire boyfriend because of what she'd read in some books."

Tyler turns away and hangs his head, but I can see his smile grow.

Kiki folds her arms across her ample chest. "Well, after today's events I have lost *any* interest I had in hooking up with a vampire. I am still holding out for a roll in the hay with Big Foot. You know what they say, big feet, big—"

"Kiki," I squeal, swatting her on the arm.

She laughs. "So how do you join this Ankh Society? Not that I want to," she adds, glaring at me through narrowed eyes.

Tyler shuffles his boots on the plush carpet. "You have to get someone in the group to sponsor you and take you to get 'bled' a number of times."

Bile creeps up my throat and the light mood is gone. "How many times?"

"Thirteen—clever, huh?" he says sarcastically. "Your sponsor keeps track."

I put a hand to my mouth. "Did *you* . . ."

He shakes his head and his cheeks burn like they've been set on fire. "My dad did it," he says quietly. "And my mom. This was hers." He pulls out a necklace from under his shirt revealing an Egyptian ankh—the symbol of eternal life. He turns the ankh over to show us two long gauge marks on the back. "Your thirteenth vampire marks the back of one of these with its teeth. You flash this and any vampire will believe you're willing to supply them with what they need. Their guard is down, they move in close—and then you stake them."

"Wow," Kiki says. "And since you kill them they can't rat you out. It's genius."

"Let me get this straight—that necklace gives you a free pass with the vamps?"

"Yeah."

I'm not sure "genius" is the right word—"crazy" is more like it. This must be what Mom meant when she said they split with the Harkers because of their divergent methods of hunting. I'm also thinking joining the Ankh Society is probably what got Mrs. Harker killed.

It's not hard to imagine getting carried away and for-getting you were supposed to stake the vampire after hav-ing blissfully enjoyed the bite thirteen times.

I wonder if I'm right and how much Tyler knows about what really happened.

My eyes drift to his neck—what I can see above his black T-shirt looks unscarred, but I would imagine someone would take care to get bitten where the marks wouldn't be so obvious. I think about his father and his turtleneck. What is Mr. Harker hiding?

My hand drifts to my chest. "I could've used one of those today. Did you notice anything weird about the vampires in this town? I mean the ones we tackled were all, like, super vampires. And one was crawling on the ceiling!"

Tyler's eyes widen. "I've heard rumors about wall-crawlers, but I've never seen one."

"*That's* the one that bit her," Kiki adds.

"*Anyway,*" I continue, ignoring her, "at the second house we cleaned there were three vampires and we liter-ally got our butts kicked—in broad daylight! I've never seen vampires like this before. They were, like, turbo-charged."

"My dad thinks . . ." He looks at Kiki and me in turn as if deciding if he should go on.

"Thinks . . . ," Kiki says with a shrug.

"He thinks whatever is going on has to do with ley lines."

Kiki raises an eyebrow. "Lay lines? Is that slang for pickup lines?"

Tyler shakes his head. "*L. E. Y.* They're invisible, magnetically charged lines that circle the earth. Some people think those are the paths fairies and other supernatural creatures used to travel."

I scoff, "So you're saying *fairy paths* are responsible for the über vamps we've encountered?"

He cringes. "Look, I know it sounds stupid and I don't even know if it's true, but my dad thinks somewhere in this area is a *nexus* point—a place where a lot of the lines converge, making it a power center. He thinks something has activated the area and the negative energy is drawing vampires to the town and that could be giving them extra power—and bringing whatever it is that's going after the kids, too."

We pull into the parking lot and Mr. Harker is pacing back and forth in front of his car.

"I better go," Tyler says, eyeing his father nervously.

"Wait," Kiki says. "Is the eye-liner part of the *look*? You know for the Ankh group?"

He shakes his head.

"Oh, good," she says with relief. She leans in toward him. "It really needs to go. It doesn't work with your skin tone and you've got such nice eyes I'd hate to see them hidden by all that junk."

Tyler turns to me as if to ask if Kiki is for real.

I shrug. "You do have nice eyes, though. . . ." I turn away before I embarrass myself any more.

"And I think you should trim your hair—just a little," she continues. "You keep hiding behind it. You can still be messy, but with a little mousse or gel it'll be more of a controlled mess."

"I'll take that under consideration," he says.

"Okay, bye!" Kiki says cheerfully. "Wait! Switch phones." She holds her phone out to him and he takes it. "Put your number in."

He punches some buttons and hands it back to her.

"Give me yours," Kiki says. She puts in her own number and tosses it back to him. "Maybe we'll see you tonight."

He smiles at Kiki. "Hope so." He tilts his head at me. "Later."

He gets out of the limo and I frown. How come Kiki got a "hope so" and a smile, and all I got was a "later"?

Kiki hikes a thumb in Tyler's direction. "Play your cards right and he's your boob guy."

"I think he's more interested in *your* boobs."

"Please! Didn't you see the way he kept checking you out?"

"No."

She hikes her cami up. "I did."

I roll my eyes thinking that's not likely. "Whatever."

"Are you mad about something?"

My stomach turns and I'm not sure what I'm feeling. "No. I'm just wiped out."

"Well, a soak in the hot tub will make you feel better. Do you think Tyler will ditch the guy-liner? I hope so—he really does have gorgeous eyes."

I nod and realize I'm feeling jealous—jealous of Kiki and her boobs, and how easily she can talk to Tyler and get people to do things her way. And it's only a matter of time before she'll get bored of hunting and move on to her next *calling*.

And I'll be alone again.

"Hey, do you want to sleep over tonight?" she asks.

"Sleep over?"

"Yeah, you know, you bring your pj's and a toothbrush and stay over at my house."

A lightness fills me and chases away my dark mood. "Sure."

A smile breaks out on my face and she grins in return. "Cool! We can look at new stakes online and some new hunting clothes. I'd really like the company, too. Sam doesn't stay over and I keep having these bad dreams. I wake up and feel like there's something in my room. . . ." Her face clouds over. "Whispering."

My blood runs cold as I hear the words I'd dreamed in my head as clear as a bell.

Revenge. Hunger. Feed.

Suddenly there is a knock on the window to my right, making me jump. Mom is standing on the other side—her eyes on fire. "Daphne Anne Van Helsing, what the hell were you doing in this car with that boy?"

9.

I open the door and Mom practically drags me out by the arm. "I told you to stay away from him and then what do I see when we head into the parking lot? Tyler Harker getting out of this . . . this *limo* with you inside. What were you thinking?"

"Joy," Dad says, stepping between us. "Take it easy."

Kiki hurriedly follows me out. "I'm sorry, Mr. and Mrs. Van Helsing; it was my idea to give him a ride. Daphne even told me she wasn't supposed to be with him." Kiki gives them major puppy-eyes. "It won't happen again."

Mom glares at her for a second then her dark eyes dart back to mine. "You don't want to mess with the Harkers — either one of you. You have no idea the things they're into."

I want to tell her we know all about the Harkers' twisted methods, but I'm thinking now isn't a good time. I glance at Kiki who has diverted her attention to moving some small rocks around on the pavement with her foot. I haven't had a chance to tell Kiki about what happened to Mrs. Harker, so I'm glad she's sensed she shouldn't be running her mouth about the Ankh Society in front of my mother.

"Mom, there's something really strange about the vampires here," I start, changing the subject.

She nods. "We know. We would've called you but both of our phones inexplicably died after we drove over a bridge on our way to our first house; they won't even hold a charge now. But yes, the vampires here are unbelievably strong. We thought the first one we encountered was an anomaly, but after our second house we tried to locate you so we could warn you."

I notice Mom is looking a little roughed-up. Her jacket sleeve is slightly torn at the shoulder and there's brownish fingerlike marks on her wrist that I'm guessing came from a vampire gripping her hard. Dad's faced is flushed and sweaty, and his sparse hair is tangled, making him look a little like a mad scientist.

"Your mother and I went to your first house to see if you were okay and we were greatly relieved to find the cleanup crew there who let us know you'd been in touch and had finished your second house. They told us you were heading back here."

Mom glances toward Mr. Harker's car. "And not with the either of the Harkers." She turns to Kiki. "Ms. Crusher, in light of the unusual circumstances I will have to insist you find some other way to entertain yourself. You may have thought this was some sort of a game, but it's not safe for you to continue working with Daphne."

Dad nods. "I have to agree; surely you can see that it's too dangerous."

Kiki looks up at Mom and Dad. "One could also say it's not safe for Daphne to continue working *alone*." She puts a hand on one hip. "After what I saw today, I honestly can't believe you'd let her go out hunting by herself even if the vampires weren't all jacked-up. And *look* at Daphne; you didn't even ask if she was okay. And I thought *my* parents were bad," she mutters.

My stomach drops as Dad hangs his head and Mom's eyes widen in surprise.

Mom's face freezes into an expressionless mask. "Of course she's okay. Daphne knows what she's—"

"If I hadn't been with Daphne she might have gotten killed today," Kiki interrupts. "I may not have the experience you all have, but it's clear hunting vampires is not something *anyone* should do solo—let alone someone our age."

Mom's mouth drops and for once she is actually speechless.

"Daphne is going to come to my house to unwind for a bit," Kiki continues. "Maybe you all can figure out what's going on so when we continue hunting this evening we'll be better prepared. Oh, and she's spending the night too."

Mom stares at Kiki, her face drained of color save for two red spots on her cheeks. "Who do you think you're talking to, Ms. Crush—"

Dad holds out a hand, cutting Mom off. "I think taking some time off is a good idea, Doodlebug. Your mom and I bought disposable cell phones, why don't you come to our room and I'll give you the numbers."

Mom glares at him but remains quiet.

"Um, all right." I look at Kiki who's sporting a small, but triumphant smile. "Do you want to wait in my room?"

"Sure."

I fish through my purse until I find my key card. She takes it and gives Mom one last withering glare.

As Kiki stalks to my room, Mom looks after her and folds her arms across her chest. "That girl has a lot of nerve. But I guess that's what it takes to want to go out with you tonight."

"It's a good thing she was with me today." I wait for Mom to ask what happened or comment on my appearance, but after Kiki enters my room she turns to me, all business.

"Well, let's get on with it. We have to do some online research into why the vampires in this area might be stronger than normal and look into the other problem. I'm leaning toward my original theory of a psychic vampire— perhaps a pediatric doctor or nurse. Officer MacCready got us the addresses of each victim and their doctors' names so we can map them and look for a pattern the police might have missed."

She looks up into the afternoon sky—clear blue now that morning fog has burnt away. "I just wish we'd been more successful with the house-cleaning today. Apparently the Harkers are done and asking for a shot at the remainder of our list."

"It will be okay," Dad says gently. "Things always work out."

She doesn't respond and starts walking toward our rooms. There are so many things I want to ask about the Harkers using the Ankh Society ruse to clean houses— and if it backfired and got Mrs. Harker killed.

"Mom?"

She turns to me—no expression on her face. "Yes?" she says testily.

I hang my head. "Nothing."

Dad looks my way and gives me a smile.

"Actually, Tyler said his dad was going to check out something called ley lines, spelled l-e-y. He thought that might have something to do with what's going on and I guess it wouldn't hurt to check it out."

Mom looks down her nose at me. "What else did Tyler tell you?"

"Nothing. Kiki did most of the talking."

She juts her chin out. "Good. We'll check out these ley lines, but it sounds like another wild-goose chase coming from a very disturbed man."

I nod, but when it comes to hunting vampires—disturbed or not—the Harkers are kicking our butts.

After I talk with my parents I knock on my door. Kiki opens it, and my stomach lurches when I see my binder in her hands. I snatch it from her. *"Are you going through my things?"*

"Chill out! I was just bored and noticed you had some magazines in that crate." She rolls her eyes. "When I saw it was *Jennifer-Kate* I kept digging to see if you had anything better. I thought the binder might have some slaying info."

"Well, it doesn't!"

Kiki waves a hand at me. "*Relax*, I thought the pictures where cute, but I wish you hadn't made me look like I swallowed a beach ball—I wasn't *that* fat."

My cheeks flush and I stuff the binder in my crate. "I was little, okay?"

She laughs. "I'm just giving you shit. I was actually really psyched you drew me instead of Sugar."

I tilt my chin down and then give her a sideways look. "So you don't think it's incredibly lame?"

"What, that you drew a picture of me—of us?"

I nod.

"No. What's incredibly lame is your parents not taking one of those metro jobs you told me about so you wouldn't have to drive around the country like a gang of vampire-killing hobos." She shakes her head. "While you were gone I got to thinking. I know you said your parents are all about helping small towns like this one, but shouldn't their priorities have changed when they had you?"

I sigh. "One does tend to wonder."

She curls her lip in disdain. "It's the exact same thing with my parents. It's all about the work. I mean nobody forced them to rock out with the toddler set or, in your case, kill vampires. Seriously—why?"

I don't have an answer, but I'm beyond glad Kiki is

giving a voice to all of my concerns—it makes me feel less crazy. "I can't believe what you said to my parents before. Thanks."

Kiki lowers herself on my bed. "It was actually very cathartic. It's a variation on the *'What the hell were you thinking?'* speech I never had the nerve to give my parents. When they replaced me with Sugar they didn't even ask how I felt, they just stated it wasn't *personal* and the decision was driven by *'the numbers.'* They never even asked if I was okay with it—and I wasn't." She purses her lips. "What do 'numbers' mean to a five-year-old anyway?"

She rolls her eyes. "Our parents have this tunnel vision; all they think about is how many vampires they need to kill or what share of the TV ratings they scored—you and I are just part of getting the job done."

She walks over to the dresser and takes my binder out of the crate. She flips through until she gets to the picture I drew of us and taps a finger on each of the musical notes I'd drawn. "I sometimes think I've been afraid to confront my parents because they'll confirm what I suspect—that I really am secondary to The Disco Unicorn Empire."

I look at us standing side by side in the mirror—our expressions marked with confusion and sadness. "I know what you mean."

Her eyes find mine in the mirror. She nods. "I could

see it in your face at the bar last night. I think that's why I followed you outside. I just knew we were kindred spirits."

Who would have thought a washed-up child star and a fourth generation vampire slayer would be "kindred spirits." I leaf through the pages of my binder. "All these pictures—they're of girls I was hoping to meet, hoping to be friends with. You were the only real person I drew."

A slow smile comes to her face. "Apparently, you and I were predestined to slay vampires together. It's fate."

I grimace, thinking about Mr. Harker and all of his talk about fate. "When I drew this I was really hoping to leave vampires behind and move into the Pink Pony Playhouse and eat pineapple pizza."

"Trust me; the Pink Pony Playhouse isn't all it's cracked up to be. Unicorn shit smells the same as horse's."

I look around my room. "It's got to be better than this."

"Get cleaned up and I'll show you where the real Disco Unicorns get away to—and there isn't a hint of pink."

Sam pulls the limo up to Kiki's "cottage" which is really a three-story Chinese pagoda overlooking the Damariscotta River. The edges of the rooflines curve up toward the sky and are lined with intricate carvings and brightly colored lattice work. Dragons perch on each of the corners with their open mouths above the down spouts. A tall finial on the top with its budlike tip shines in the sun. Gardens filled with white, smooth stones line the driveway leading up to the wooden front steps. Two large marble statues depicting some sort of lionlike creatures with open mouths and sharp teeth flank the steps and I can see the river in the back with twisted pines dotting the shore. It feels like I stepped out of the limo into coastal China.

"This is where you live?"

"Yep. A retired sea captain who had spent a lot of time in Asia built it in the early 1800s. It was empty for something like seventy years before my parents spotted it when they were kayaking on the river and had it restored. I have to warn you," she says as Sam opens the limo door for us, "my parents went a little overboard with the decor. It's all the weird stuff they've collected from around the world."

"No unicorn wallpaper?"

She wrinkles her nose. "That stuff is all at our Hollywood Hills house where they get interviewed a lot. This place is full of tribal masks, architectural pieces recovered from old temples and churches, and a favorite of my mom's—fertility statues. When my parents aren't sporting unicorn horns and rapping the alphabet, they're one hundred percent new-age hippie. The tabloids would have a field day if they saw the obscene amount of giant stone breasts, swollen bellies, and erect penises around the house. It's all crap, though; I am an only child after all."

"Do you need help with your things?" Sam asks me.

I look down at my crate and duffel bag. "I'm okay, thanks."

Kiki picks up my crate. "We'll be good until sunset."

"Very good, Ms. Crusher." Sam nods to me and he makes his way to a small sports car parked next to the Cadillac he'd driven last night.

"Let's get some lunch and head for the hot tub!"

I sling my duffel bag strap over my shoulder and follow Kiki up the front steps. She unlocks the front door and steps in. Tucking my crate under one arm, she walks with a hand held out and spins a series of twelve ornate cylinders hanging in a row on the wall. She puts the crate down, turns to me with a serene look on her face, and clasps her hands as if in prayer. *"Om mani padme hum."*

"Huh?"

"What is your heart's desire?"

I raise an eyebrow. "What?"

She laughs. "They're Tibetan prayer wheels; inside each one the mantra *'Om mani padme hum'* is written over and over again on paper. When you spin the wheel it's kind of like your prayers are multiplied by a million. It's supposed to invoke the benevolent attention and blessings of *Chenrezig*, the Hindu embodiment of compassion."

"Okay."

"Yeah, I know—more crap. But these are from an actual Tibetan temple. My parents had them installed a few months ago. But name your heart's desire, spin the wheel, and with some luck, Chenrezig will grant your wish."

I look at the wheels. My first thought is the means to retire from slaying, but that's not going to happen anytime soon, so I decide to wish for something more realistic. I reach my hand out and touch the first one. It almost feels like there's a faint of hum of electricity inside. "May we prove triumphant against the crazed vampires of South Bristol, protect the children from their unknown predator, and rejuvenate our weary muscles in the hot tub."

I make my way down the line, spinning each wheel. When I meet up with Kiki at the end she cocks her head toward a doorway. "Kitchen is this way. Are you sure I can't convince you to have a drink? Maybe some champagne to celebrate the fact we're still alive?"

"We need to be on our game tonight. No champagne."

She puts her hands on her hips, looking deadly serious. "All the really cool vampire hunters follow up kills with champagne."

I can't help but smile. "I tell you what—if we get more vamps than the Harkers tonight I'll take you up on that."

"That's my girl. It's time to forget your parents' way of slaying and embrace the new age."

"What do new-age slayers have for lunch?"

"Everyone knows the really cool slayers are partial to nachos."

"I think I'm going to like being a really cool slayer."

10.

After some killer nachos, Kiki
takes me up to the third floor of the pagoda. It's one big
open space with floor-to-ceiling windows all around. A
simple woven rug sits in the middle of the polished wood
floors, and large, brightly colored pillows are scattered
here and there against the walls of the otherwise empty
room.

"My parents come up here to meditate and do yoga."
She grimaces. "Once I think they were doing—*it*."

I mirror her grimace and then turn slowly, taking in
the three-hundred-sixty-degree view. "Wow."

To the north of the house, an old stone church steeple
is peeking through the trees in the distance. To the south

is a wide lawn sloping down to the river. A skinny rock, maybe ten feet tall, stands sentry in the middle of the lawn surrounded by another garden lined with white stones. Across the river in direct line with the house, is an outcrop of jumbled boulders covered with stunted pines, their exposed roots looking desperately for purchase in the inhospitable terrain.

Kiki walks toward the windows facing the river. "This is why I like to stay here." She puts a hand on the window and takes a deep breath. "No matter how crazy things get in California, just looking out these windows grounds me and I can pretend my parents aren't billionaire kiddie-rock stars."

I watch the river tumble by, carrying logs and various ducks as it goes. The knots in my stomach unravel as I take in the tranquil view. "This is really nice."

She sighs. "But we can't forget we have a big job ahead of us tonight. Let's hit the hot tub and strategize."

I watch a duck with a rounded black and white head dive under water. "Okay," I say when it pops back up. "But I don't have a suit."

"We don't need suits."

My face flushes and Kiki laughs. "We have a bunch of extra suits we bought for shy guests. You can have your pick."

"Thanks. I think I need to take the new-age slayer stuff one step at a time."

I follow her down the spiral staircase wishing we could stay up here long enough to forget I'm a vampire slayer.

"I'll meet you outside," Kiki calls out from the other side of the bathroom door.

"Sure." I go back to staring at myself in the mirror. I'm as pale as a vampire, but sporting this designer two-piece I can almost imagine myself in the pages of *Jennifer-Kate*'s swimsuit edition. Of course I have nothing on Kiki, who had unabashedly gotten changed in front of me, was tan, and totally rocked a Swarovski crystal-studded bikini she put on.

And then there is the trail of raw claw marks on my chest. Not exactly fashion forward.

Given a choice, it's no wonder Tyler was smiling at Kiki and not me.

Not that I really care.

I head out and wind my way past the masks flanking the walls that are totally creeping me out. Some have strange shells for eyes that give the appearance the eye sockets have been sewn shut. Others have jagged bone teeth and tufts of what looks like real human hair jutting out from their wooden chins. Grotesque statues with twisted faces and engorged body parts glare at me from dark corners of the rooms.

I simply can't reconcile the image of Kiki's parents singing in their pastel unicorn costumes with people who find these disturbing collectibles appealing. But maybe this macabre menagerie is what helps Kiki push The Disco Unicorns out of her mind.

A large, jewel-encrusted prayer wheel is mounted by the French doors leading out to the patio. I give it a good spin. "May my heart's desire come true," I whisper. I turn the wheel a second time for extra luck and wish I could remember the mantra Kiki had said.

I step out onto the cool blue stone patio and shiver. It's almost five thirty and the sun has dipped just behind the tree line now and my chilled, aching muscles urge me toward the warm hot tub.

Kiki beckons me in. "Hurry up—time's a wasting."

"Sorry."

She splashes water at me as I slide into the tub. "You don't need to be sorry; you just need to get in."

I slink down into the water, and the chlorine stings my cuts. Bubbles jump up and tickle my nose, but the warmth of the water brings back some of that relaxed feeling I had before. I look out at the large rock jutting up from the lawn and breathe deep. "If it weren't for all the masks and things in your house I'd move in here in a heartbeat."

"They're not so bad. When I was little I imagined they were here to protect me. I even gave them each a name. Saying hello to 'George' or 'Ashley' definitely reduced the creep factor. There are a few I avoid, but overall it's like coming home to friends I never had."

"But you're not like me—you had actual kids to play with."

She rolls her eyes. "The kids on the show abandoned me once Sugar came on board, and the ones at school only wanted to hang with me because of my parents. Once they realized I was nothing special they drifted off too."

"I always wanted to go to school," I say longingly.

She scoffs. "School sucks. Granted I didn't make it a full year, but I had all these big plans to be 'normal' and try out for cheerleading and shit like that. Of course starting school at age twelve was a huge mistake. Twelve-year-old girls are the definition of 'suck'! But with my dance background I thought I was a shoe-in for the cheerleading squad." She wrinkles her nose. "Apparently they didn't like chubby kids any more than the producers of the Pink Pony Playhouse."

"But what about high school? Don't you think it'd be

fun to go to the prom? You know, dress up in a gown, dance with some incredibly hot guy, and then take a limo to a hotel afterward. . . ." I trail off, not ready to share my prom fantasy with Kiki.

"It sounds nice, Daphne, but all of the guys I meet are jerks who want me to pay for everything because they know my parents are rich. And I've had my fill of fancy dresses and limo rides—unless they're used to take me to my next vampire."

"I don't get it, Kiki; why *do* you want to hunt vampires? Especially after what happened today."

She shrugs. "What else am I going to do? Other than singing and dancing—something no one wants to pay me to do—I have no marketable skills. And what's wrong with wanting to help people? That's a hell of a lot better than having a multiplatinum record, right?"

"You could work with orphans in one of a gazillion needy places, or feed the poor, or read to old people."

"Anybody could do that stuff, but like I said before, the second you killed that vampire behind The Rusty Rudder, I knew I'd finally found my calling."

"If you say so."

"Look, I know you're all disenchanted with the biz, but think about all the lives you've saved."

"If I quit there's always going to be some lunatic who

will take my . . ." Kiki is glaring at me. "I mean *eager* new slayer who will take my place."

"Maybe you're burned out and you need a vacation. Or . . ." She sits up, her eyes glittering. "You need to remember how it felt to kill your first vampire. My parents are totally into this thing called 'talk therapy.' I'll walk you through it and see if I can help you get your mojo back."

"*I don't want my mojo back.* I want to go to school, eat lunch in a cafeteria, and go to prom! I want a house and a dog and a goldfish and a room where I can hang posters on the walls."

"*I hear you saying* you don't want your mojo back," she says serenely.

I give her a pained look. "This is stupid."

"*I hear you saying* you think talk therapy is stupid."

I bury my head in my hands. "This isn't going to help my rediscover my love for slaying."

"*I hear you saying* you once *loved* slaying."

I give a start and look up. "No! I mean maybe I did . . . a little, when I was little. But I was a delusional kid living in a fantasy world."

"How old were you when you killed your first vampire?"

I look her in the eye. "I killed my first vampire around the same time you were trying out for cheerleading."

"I hear you—"

"Please stop that."

She holds her hands up. "Fine. Tell me about your first kill," she says placidly.

"It's not a pretty story."

"That's okay. Just talk."

"Fine. After my senile grandfather was taken away—for staking a nonvampire . . ."

Kiki's eyes widen.

"My parents had been bringing me along to all the police briefings and, by the time I was ten, house-cleanings, so I could learn the family business. I was twelve when we got called to Oak Hill, Arkansas, population twenty-eight, for a do-it-in-your-sleep kind of job. The cops were supposed to call for a lockdown using the 'felons on the loose' story that's protocol in cases like this to keep people from unwittingly inviting any vampires into their homes."

"Go on," she says encouragingly, like a talk-show host pumping her guests to spill their guts.

"After a twenty-hour nonstop drive, we arrived just after dusk and Sheriff Jeffries welcomed us into his cement-block office for a briefing. Unfortunately, while we were on our way, Jeffries and his second-in-command got themselves turned. They closed the door to the office and jumped us."

Kiki winces and totally blows her pseudo-psychiatrist-judgment-free facade. "Ouch."

"Yup. Jeffries went right for Dad's throat. Mom was fending off the other guy so I knew it was up to me to help my dad. I grabbed the knife I'd recently started wearing and with the help of crazy amounts of adrenaline, I managed to separate a good deal of Jeffries's neck from his body. When he finally fell, my dad was staring at me. Blood was gushing from under his chin. His shirt was soaked. His eyes rolled up and he fell to the floor.

"Jeffries—even with his esophagus severed and his head bent back at an unnatural angle—started to drag his sorry undead ass across the tiles to where my dad was lying. Without thinking, I grabbed a stake from Mom's bag and plunged it into his chest and I hit a home run my very first time. I used my knife to hack the rest of his neck off and make a clean break.

"I turned back to my dad and my mother was stitching his wound shut. With each loop of thread, the skin was drawn back against his neck and I was feeling good because I knew everything was going to be okay. But when she was done she fell on his chest, crying and begging him not to leave us.

"Seeing my mom like that, well, I felt like I'd been punched in the stomach, and for the first time I realized

my parents had left out a crucial part of the 'hunting vampires' scenario. They'd neglected to tell me it was kill or
be killed."

I look her in the eyes. "Did I mention I was twelve?"

Kiki stares at me with her mouth open.

"So you could say my first kill wasn't a kick-ass cool
adrenaline rush. It was more like *I'm a kid and it just dawned
on me that at any time my parents could be killed, I would be an
orphan, and they don't seem to care.*"

I fold my arms across my chest and sink down until
my chin is just above the water. I close my eyes and tor-
ture myself by playing the Oak Hill scene over again in
my head.

"I'm sorry, Daphne. I didn't know."

I purse my lips in an effort to steel myself against the
tears gathering in my eyes.

"You need to talk to them," she says. "You need to find
out why they're doing it; otherwise it's just going to keep
eating at you."

I sit up and sniff. The cool air bites at my chest. "What
about you? You told my parents off, but can you do it to
yours?"

She shakes her head. "Easier said than done. I've
always been afraid the truth will just make me feel worse."

"I know what you mean."

Kiki turns and her eyes widen as she looks out toward the river. "Hey, is that Tyler?" She stands up and points down toward the shore "I think it is, and he's got some sort of stick."

I get up and squint. Tyler Harker and his father are walking along the river's edge. They have their heads down and they're both holding something sticklike that bobs along with each step they take. "What are they doing?"

"I have no clue." She waves her hands over her head. *"Tyler! Up here!"*

He jerks his head up in surprise.

She cups her hands to her mouth like a megaphone. *"What are you doing down there?"*

I swat her arm. "Kiki, stop! Remember what my mom said."

"How is your mother going to know you were with Tyler?" She pulls on her bikini straps, making her large breasts move up and down. "And maybe we can use our feminine wiles to get some info that'll help team Van Helsing."

I look down at my bathing suit, knowing I don't have as much to work with as Kiki. I turn back to shore where Tyler is conferring with his father. Mr. Harker nods, points the end of whatever he's holding in our direction, and then the two of them head our way.

"Oh, shit." I hop out of the tub and grab a towel and wrap it around me, making sure I've got my bite marks covered up.

"You're hiding your feminine wiles," she chastises as she tries to pull my towel off.

I slap at her hands. "Stop it!"

"Fine! I guess I'll have to do the dirty work."

I hug the towel tighter around me and as they get closer and I see they're each gripping some of sort of wooden dowel with a stiff wire a little over a foot long attached.

Tyler's eyes widen as he takes Kiki in. "Dad, this is Kiki—she's the one who gave me a ride back to the motel."

Mr. Harker grunts but his focus is on the large stone rock jutting out from the garden. "I knew we were on the right track. The lines don't lie," he says to no one in particular. He takes a few steps and the wire in his hand points toward the ground as if tugged by an invisible force. "They're all converging here. This is the nexus point."

He points to the stone. "Do you see that, boy? That's the *standing stone*. You'll find tall stones jutting out of the earth like this wherever multiple lines converge." He looks to the river. "There," he says, his eyes watering up. His lip quivers as he points a shaking finger straight in front of him, his eyes glued to the outcrop across the water. "That's where they hunt from. That's where I'll find her," he whispers. He turns to me and I step back. "And finding you here is just icing on the cake. It's all coming together like it was predestined."

Tyler looks like he'd be more than happy to have the earth swallow him up, and Kiki's face is screwed up like someone just handed her a rotten egg. She picks up her towel and wraps it around herself. I'm pretty sure she's regretting her decision to work her feminine wiles on the likes of Nathan Harker.

Mr. Harker holds the wire out and circles the big rock. "I've waited so long," he mutters as he stops and gazes out across the water again. "But I've finally found it."

Kiki clears her throat. "Um, what exactly did you find, sir?"

Mr. Harker grins at her like a mad hatter. "Probably the greatest nexus point in the country; they run along the earth's magnetic fields and are a source of great power. That stone marks a convergence of many lines. Follow a straight path north from the rock. There's this house, and then the church. It's no coincidence where they've been placed. The builders instinctively followed the line to capitalize on the energy."

He holds out the rod to Kiki. "I can see in your eyes you don't believe, but take this, it's a dowsing rod. Take it and you'll see I'm right."

Kiki slowly reaches out her hand and reluctantly takes the rod.

"You gotta walk or it won't work, but circle this rock and you'll feel it."

She gives me a *what-have-I-gotten-myself-into* look, and then starts to walk. The metal tip suddenly plunges toward the ground and she gasps. "Oh," she says in astonishment. "I can feel this fuzzy sort of tingle moving up my arm." As she continues around the stone, the tip rises and falls every few steps.

Mr. Harker grins. "Every time you pass a ley line the rod will be attracted to it."

"Could these lines disrupt a cell phone?" I ask.

"Absolutely. I've found ley lines before but never this powerful."

I nod and wonder if Mom's and Dad's phones died crossing a line.

Kiki laughs every time the rod dips down. "This is so amazing. Daphne, you have to try it."

She rushes over to me, pushes the rod in my hand and pulls me toward the rock. The rod jerks down, and my hand begins to tingle. I turn to Mr. Harker. "I think I—"

He absentmindedly tugs down his collar and my stomach twists in horror. Mr. Harker's neck is ravaged by bite marks. There are fresh wounds side-by-side with round, pearly white scars in sets of two.

Unlike Tyler, Mr. Harker is obviously letting the vampires feed on him before he stakes them.

I catch Tyler looking at me with pained eyes. He hangs his head in embarrassment and my heart breaks for him. It's obvious Mr. Harker is a very troubled man and I can only imagine what it's been like for Tyler cooped up in his car or random hotel with no one to talk to but his vampire-junkie father.

I realize Mr. Harker is staring at me waiting for me to elaborate on what I'd started to say. I swallow. "Um, yeah, I can definitely feel something." I hand the dowsing rod back to Mr. Harker, unable to look him in the eye. I notice the ring he'd been playing with in Officer MacCready's office yesterday. It's on his wedding finger, but it's engraved with symbols much like the prayer wheels.

"So you believe me now?" he asks.

"Uh, yeah. I guess."

"Totally!" Kiki adds. "But I'm not sure what having a bunch of ley lines around means."

His eyes bore into hers and she takes a few shuffling steps backward. "It means this place is the source of all the trouble."

Kiki frowns and readjusts her towel. "My house is responsible for bringing super vampires to South Bristol?"

He ignores her and I gasp as he reaches out and grips my wrist. "You gotta tell your parents what you've seen. Tell them everything." He moves in closer to me and his rancid breath almost makes me choke. "Tell them we gotta stick together. Work on your dad; I know he's receptive. You have to change their minds. You *have* to," he says, squeezing my wrist painfully.

"Dad!" Tyler says. "Stop." He puts his hand on his father's and Mr. Harker releases me.

Mr. Harker turns to Tyler and starts rocking back and forth on his feet. "The moon's not right. It's not time yet. I've got to check the charts. But it's almost sunset. We best be going and get ready to work. We have to make top dollar tonight. We have to prepare for your future."

Without saying good-bye, Mr. Harker starts down the lawn toward the river. When his father gets out of earshot Tyler turns to us. "Look up *the lamia*—that's what my dad thinks is hunting the children," he says hurriedly. "He has a lot of crazy ideas about things, but after finding these ley lines, I think he may be on to something."

"Tyler!" his father calls out. "We need to move."

He starts to leave, but then turns back and takes my hands in his. "If I find out anything else I'll let you know."

I can hardly breathe as I look up into his blue eyes. I nod and my mouth twitches as I force it into a smile. "Um, I'll be on patrol downtown after sunset; I'm sure we'll run into you. Except if my mom is around we won't be able to talk. But I'm sleeping here at Kiki's tonight. You should come over." I look at Kiki to see if that's all right and she nods.

He squeezes my hands gently and an electric charge runs through me. "Okay. I'll do that—if I can."

He rushes to meet up with his father and when they round a bend in the river Kiki turns to me. "Did you just make a date with Tyler Harker?"

I stare at her. "Oh, my God. Did I?"

"You did, you rebel."

"I did. Oh, my God, why did I do that?"

She laughs. "Take a deep breath."

"What was I thinking?"

"That he's cute and since he ditched the guy-liner he's totally dateable. Better hope your mom doesn't find out, but she won't hear it from me."

A million butterflies swirl around in my stomach.

"But there is something seriously wrong with Mr. Harker," she continues. "And what the hell is up with the freaking ley line? You felt something, didn't you?"

"Yeah, I did. Apparently you're living in weird-energy

central." I realize I'm shivering and drape my towel over my shoulders. "Did you see Mr. Harker's neck?"

Kiki grimaces. "There were fresh wounds. He's got to be letting them bite him before . . ." She puts a hand to her throat and shudders.

"That's what I was thinking too."

"Let's get changed and do some research before we go back to your motel."

"I'll call my dad and give him the heads-up about what Mr. Harker said. Maybe he can sneak away from my mother and talk to him."

"Let's do it." Kiki heads toward the house and opens the door for me. As she follows me in, she spins the prayer wheel. "This is going to be an interesting night."

11.

Kiki and I ride from the motel back to her house in a somber mood. Not only did my mother have a complete fit when we told her we'd been with the Harkers, but she also informed us that even though two infants had mysteriously died in their sleep the night before she was only interested in cleaning out the vampires and moving on. No doubt to get as far away from Nathan Harker as possible.

Kiki takes a swig a water bottle and screws the cap back on. "For someone hell-bent on one-upping the Harkers, your mother is surprisingly bullheaded. She wouldn't even consider the lamia as a possibility. And then to go and bag the whole thing . . ."

After what Kiki and I discovered online about the lamia I couldn't exactly blame my mother for being doubtful. Demons leaving hell to fly through the night so they can prey on infants is a little hard to swallow. I do wonder how much of her protests come from not being willing to believe Mr. Harker could possibly be right.

"Well, you heard her—she just wants to concentrate on the vampire problem and then blow out of town." Which means no more Kiki—or Tyler. I let out a long sigh. "But she did have a good point; if something as crazy as the lamia are true, how would we even attempt to stop something like that?"

"Or even find them?"

I lean back into the leather seat. "It's just hard to give up, knowing innocent babies might pay the price."

Kiki sits up. "Who says *we* have to give up? Your parents said they weren't sure you should go house-cleaning tomorrow because of the jacked-up vampires—something I would like to think I had a hand in, thank you very much. But we could go to this shop in Portland that sells magic stuff and see if the owner could help us out. It's pretty hard-core with the black arts and such—Wiccans need not apply."

I raise my eyebrows and she shrugs. "I went through a Goth phase—tried to magic my parents into quitting the biz. You can see how well that worked. Add 'witch' to the list of things I suck at. But the owner was always talking about the weirdest shit. He's definitely the go-to guy if you want information about demons."

"I guess I'm up for any excuse to get me out of slaying vampires for a day."

"Okay, then, we'll have Sam take us tomorrow; it's only an hour and a half south of here. But speaking of vampires—are we clear about our game plan for tonight?"

I nod. Kiki really must have gotten to my parents because all of sudden they're expressing some concern for my safety instead of the usual "We know you can take care of yourself" deal. Kiki and I will just patrol the main drag tonight with an emphasis of checking out the patrons of The Rusty Rudder for possible vampires. Of course Mom couldn't help but repeatedly remind us that we need a high number of kills to make coming all the way to South Bristol worthwhile—and perhaps best the Harkers' stellar numbers.

"I'm not sure I like the idea of dressing up to attract vampires though," I say.

"It's only a variation on what the Harkers are doing. We'll just make ourselves look available and hopefully the vampires will come to us and we won't get our asses kicked again."

"What if I don't fit into your mother's clothes?"

She looks me up and down. "I'm guessing you're a size four—and while your torso is a little longer than my mom's, I think her stuff will fit you like a glove."

"Maybe you should quit the vampire biz to be a stylist."

She smiles. "Who says I can't do both?"

An hour later I'm sitting in front of a mirror while Kiki finishes curling my hair. I'm wearing an actual designer dress her mother wore on a red carpet and with Kiki's expert makeup application I look like I could actually be in the pages of *Jennifer-Kate* magazine. "What if I get blood on this dress—or rip it?"

"My mother never wears the same thing twice—she won't even know it's gone."

She lets another perfect spiral curl drop from the iron, and I admire my hair. "I imagined if I went to a prom I'd do my hair just like this."

She picks up another section of my hair and rolls it around the wand. "I saw that tuxedo picture in your binder. Just how long have you been obsessed with the prom anyway?"

I glare at her in the mirror. "Who doesn't dream of going to the prom?"

"Me."

"Well, sorry I haven't had as many opportunities to get all glammed up and have guys falling all over me like you have."

She lets the next curl fall and puts the iron down. "You're totally ready for your own booty call."

I stand up and Kiki moves next to me. We both have smoky eyes and dark lips. Kiki is wearing a short denim skirt and low-cut pink sweater showing off her ample cleavage. I'm wearing a form-fitting black dress and I can hardly believe it's me I'm looking at in the mirror. "Look at us! If only it was a booty call we're after instead of vampires."

She wiggles her eyebrows up and down. "With Tyler on the prowl, who says you can't have both?"

I scoff and roll my eyes. "Who says Tyler is even into me? He could be coming over to swap slaying tips."

"Oh, please. It's so completely obvious he has the hots for you."

I put my hands on my hips. "I think he's more into you. He's always staring at your chest."

She puts her hands on her breasts. "Daphne, when your boobs are as big as mine *everyone* stares. But he didn't take my hands in his and *longingly* look into my eyes."

My stomach flutters. "Do you really think he might be interested?"

"Without a doubt."

My shoulders slump. "Even if he does like me, when this job is over we'll never see each other again. Not to mention the fact that my parents have forbidden me to have anything to do with him."

Kiki bites her lip. "You're almost eighteen. Maybe it's time you take charge of your own destiny."

My pulse quickens. "I couldn't leave my parents. I mean what would I do? Where would I even live?"

"Let's just get through tonight and let tomorrow bring its own surprises. Besides, the really important thing right now is which stakes best complete our looks," she says.

We walk over to her bed where the FedEx box of designer stakes is open. Kiki pulls out one with carved roses on the shaft and mimics staking someone. "This feels so much better than those clunkers you use."

She hands it to me and I walk to the mirror. I grip it with both hands and strike a pose.

"No," Kiki says. She takes one of my "fence post" stakes out of my duffel bag and hands it to me. "This is more you."

"So you're saying big and clunky is more me?"

She grins. "Look at yourself in the mirror. You look killer-hot."

"Is that a good thing?"

"Totally! And wait until Tyler sees you tonight. *Booty call!*"

I shiver with anticipation, but at the same time my stomach turns nervously. "Kiki, I've never kissed anyone before—what if I totally suck at it? Not that I'm saying I even want to kiss him and not that I'm saying he wants to kiss me."

She rolls her eyes. "It's the kind of thing that you don't even need to think about. Just relax and let whatever happens happen."

"I hardly know him—and this morning I kind of hated him."

"There is no timetable for falling in love."

"I'm not falling in love!"

She arches one eyebrow. "Be that as it may—love can build over time or it can hit you like a bolt of lightning. Go into this with zero expectations. Best-case scenario you get your boobs felt up, and we cross it off your list."

"May I suggest you don't put writing a romance novel on your bucket list—you're way too jaded."

"I'm not going to argue with you about that, but you could do a hell of a lot worse than Tyler Harker. My first time was with a dancer who wasn't sure if he was gay. He was. But let's go out tonight and clean up the town and if something else develops—fab for you."

We fist bump and Kiki laughs. "We are so out-vamp-
ing the Harkers tonight."

Sam opens the limo door and I hit the sidewalk with a new
air of confidence. Who knew a designer dress and kick-ass
hair could be so empowering. A slim crescent of the moon
hangs in the star-filled sky and I breathe in the salty air.

"Watch your back, Sam," Kiki tells him.

"Will do, Ms. Crusher," he says, and I know he'll keep
the car doors locked tight tonight.

"Let me check in with my parents and then we can get
started." I take my phone out and dial up Dad. "Hey, we
just got into town. We got kind of a late start."

"Okay, Doodlebug. Your mom and I are just staying
with a family until the task force arrives. They're a little
upset about the decapitated bodies in their living room,
but at least no one was hurt."

My eyes drift to Kiki and I can't help but smile. It's
hard to believe it was just last night that we were arguing about "armies of vampires" and she was helping me
drag a body behind the Dumpster. I recall her saying
that I'd be surprised how quickly you could learn to
trust someone—she was referring to guys, but I know
Kiki has my back.

I hear someone crying and arguing with Mom in the

background. "I'll let you go, Dad. Sounds like you've got your hands full."

"That would be an understatement. Be careful and don't take any unnecessary risks."

"We won't." I shut my phone and turn to Kiki. "Let's walk up and down the block once. Then we'll scout out behind the stores and restaurants to see if any vamps are lurking around."

Kiki throws her hair back off her shoulders and nods. "And when we get to The Rusty Rudder I should be on the lookout for anyone with a reddish tint in their eyes and a full beer, right?"

"Right. And you only see the red if the light hits them just so. But anyone really casing the place should be watched."

"Okay."

"If we think we've spotted a vamp, I'll make a big deal about leaving alone. . . ."

"And if anyone suspicious follows you, I'll text you and head out for backup."

"Okay, let's see what's going on."

We start walking down the block and Kiki unzips her bag. She puts her hand on the rose carved stake, and lets out a long sigh. "Is it just me, or does hunting vampires sound so much cooler when we're not actually doing it?"

I give her a look. "I keep telling you there is nothing cool about hunting vampires. And remember—you don't have to do this."

She straightens her spine and tightens her grip on the stake. "Hey, I'm part of Team Van Helsing and I didn't spend a ridiculous amount of money on this thing for nothing."

Two men are heading our way. They spot us and lean their heads closer and talk. "Incoming." The taller one takes out a cigarette and I relax as he takes a deep drag. "False alarm; he's breathing."

They give us each the once-over as they pass and then Kiki taps my arm. "Look."

I follow her gaze and catch a glimpse of someone disappearing into an alley between the florist and the bookstore. My heart quickens. "That could be someone who was tailing those guys."

We cautiously make our way to the alley. I've got my hand on my stake and when we turn in I see a man approaching Tyler who's holding out his ankh necklace.

"Great," I whisper. "Looks like Team Harker is going to get this one."

"Not if I can help it," Kiki says. *"Hey, vampire!"* she calls out.

The man turns to us in surprise—fangs bared.

"I think you'll like what we've got to offer better—unless you prefer skinny dudes."

"Kiki!" Tyler and I yell in unison as the man looks back and forth between us and Tyler with a puzzled expression.

She taps her neck. "That's right, come and get it," she says with a shaking voice that betrays her nervousness. Her chest heaves up and down. "I really need a, uh, fix."

The man licks his lips. "I had a feeling this was going to be my lucky night." He turns to Tyler. "Sorry, kid, I do prefer girls."

Tyler stares at us in disbelief, but as the man heads our way he takes out a knife and I know he's not giving up the kill that easily.

"Oh, God, he's coming," she whispers to me. "What do we do?"

I step in front of Kiki and hurry toward the man. "Me first," I say with my hand clutching the top of the stake in my bag. My heart pounds and I'm not sure how I can stake him while we're standing in the alley. I wish we'd thought this through a little better.

"Hey, vampire, watch out! That guy behind you has a knife," Kiki says.

The man turns to look back at Tyler who is rapidly approaching with his knife held high. Grateful for the distraction, I rush at the guy full force and knock him to the ground. He snarls as I land on him with my stake raised high.

"What the hell?" he cries out.

His dark soulless eyes lock onto mine and I strike him across the face with my stake before he has time to fight back. "Sorry, I changed my mind—I'm just not in the mood tonight!" I plunge the stake into his chest and then roll off him as his body goes limp. "Ow," I say realizing I've totally scraped my knees on the pavement. Maybe wearing a Herve Leger dress wasn't the best idea.

I look up and Tyler is standing over me. *"What do you think you're doing?"*

I push myself off the pavement and brush the grit off the back of the dress. "Same thing you were going to do."

He turns to Kiki with his hands up at his shoulder. "And *'Hey vampire'*? What is up with that?"

"I had to get his attention somehow," Kiki says. "It worked." She pokes him in the chest. "We totally smoked your ass. Round one goes to Team Van Helsing! I'll call it in, Daphne."

I nod, turn my back to Tyler, and then quickly reach under my dress for the knife strapped to my thigh. When I turn back, Tyler is staring at me. "I don't usually wear a dress for hunting," I say, blushing. I lean over the vampire and grunt as I hack his head off with five strokes.

"You really don't have to do that," he chides after I stand up and kick the head away.

Kiki shuts her phone and stares at Tyler. "You don't cut the heads off after you stake them?"

"No."

"Ha! I knew it!" she turns to me. "I told you heads can't reattach. Do you put garlic in their mouths?"

He laughs. "No. It is a pretty useful repellent, but my dad and I don't use it. And here's another thing," Tyler says looking at me. "If you're going to willingly offer yourself to a vampire you have to use a different kind of stake." He reaches into an inside pocket of his trench coat and reveals a sharpened stake no more than six inches long. "You have to use more force to get this in at close range, but it's easier to conceal and stab them with if you're in an upright position."

"Thanks for the tips," I say begrudgingly.

"We so need to go hunting with you," Kiki says.

I glare at her and she puts her hands on her hips. "And your parents need to get over whatever issues they have with the Harkers, stop the medieval practices, and start acting like twenty-first-century slayers. Think of all the money they'd save by not buying so much freaking garlic." She turns to Tyler. "You should see the ridiculous amount of garlic they have. Their hotel room reeks of it."

"Tyler!"

Mr. Harker is strutting up the alley. "Did you get that one?"

He gives us a look, barely suppressing a grin. "No. They stole this one right out from under my nose."

Mr. Harker nods and then he surveys the body. "Daphne, you can tell your parents that they don't need to cut the head off if you've staked them. Maybe they'll listen to you—they never would take my word on it."

Kiki smiles smugly.

I roll my eyes. "Okay, I get it. *One or the other*."

Mr. Harker shakes his head. "Your folks always were so damned set in their ways." He tilts his head toward Tyler. "At least we got six so far tonight. I think this area is clean. Let's go check out the park down by the waterfront. You're welcome to join us, ladies."

Kiki looks at me hopefully.

"Maybe we'll catch up with you later," I say.

Tyler smiles and doesn't seem to mind that we stole his vampire. But maybe that's because they already got six. "Yeah, I'll definitely see you later."

My stomach flip-flops.

We watch them leave the alley and I look down at the decapitated head. "That was quite the act you put on before, Kiki."

She beams. "Do you really think so? I was hoping I didn't sound too over-the-top."

"You were totally convincing. There is no doubt in my mind that vampire believed he was getting an easy meal. Hey, after the cleanup crew arrives how about we hit the pub? It sounds like the Harkers have taken care of any wandering vamps in the area."

"Can I get a drink, *Mom*?"

"I'd say that performance definitely deserves one."

Her eyes widen. "Really?"

"I'm not a total slave driver."

"Hmmm. Do you think a Bloody Mary would be too cliché?"

I wrinkle my nose. "Uh, yeah."

"What about a pomegranate martini? They're red. It could be our *signature* drink."

"All the really cool slayers have signature drinks."

Kiki laughs. "Now you're acting like a twenty-first-century slayer!"

"Let's move the body back into the shadows." I smile at her. "And this time you can get the head."

12.

We enter the bar and it's a lot less crowded than the night before. Dad has a theory that infested towns give off a vibe that keeps a lot of people close to home—kind like an instinctual survival thing. Mom has gone on the record stating that it's crap, but I think he could be right.

"Kiki!"

We turn and Gabe is sauntering over to us. "I was hoping you were going to show up. What happened to you last night?" He puts an arm around her and nuzzles into her neck. "You got me all worked up and then left me high and dry."

She ducks out from under his arm but she's smiling.

I'm thinking she likes Gabe a little more than she'll admit.

"Something came up," she tells him. "But apparently you weren't that broken up about it because you didn't call."

"I had a little too much to drink last night and today I was driving Victoria around."

Kiki scoffs. "Oh, well, maybe you can hook up with Victoria tonight."

He rolls his eyes. "Relax. She and Michael are still together. He didn't show up for work today and she asked if I could help her find him. So, can we have a do-over?"

Kiki shakes her head. "Sorry, Gabe, but Daphne and I have business stuff to take care of."

Gabe eyes me. "You were here last night, right?"

"Uh, yeah."

He looks us both up and down. "Are you two hooking up?" He smiles slyly. "Because we could make it a three-some."

My mouth drops open and Kiki swats him on the arm.

"Daphne and I are not hooking up."

Gabe cocks his head. "We could still go for it. Do you swing both ways, Daphne?"

She pushes him away. "Oh, my God! You're *such an ass*!"

"Hey, I'm sorry." He laughs. "I'm just kidding. I was trying to get you back for abandoning me last night." He looks solemnly at me. "I hope I didn't offend you, Daphne. How about I buy you both a drink to make up for my bad behavior?"

Kiki's eyes widen. "You're offering to buy? Alert the media, hell has officially frozen over."

"Hey, I figure I should start manning up in our relationship."

"We have a relationship?" Kiki deadpans.

Gabe puts a hand over his heart. "Kiki, baby, you're killing me. You know I only have eyes for you."

She smiles and a blush comes to her cheeks. "Okay, we'll have two pomegranate martinis."

Gabe bows. "Coming right up." He heads for the bar and Kiki grins after him. "Let's go sit in that booth over there."

"Are you going to have him over tonight?" I ask, thinking a booty call with Gabe will definitely put a wet blanket on my first sleepover.

She takes a sugar packet from the table and opens it up. "I'm thinking that keeping him at arm's length might be just the thing to take our relationship to the next level, but . . ." She tilts her head back and pours the sugar in her mouth.

I cringe. "Ew."

"I just needed a little pick-me-up." She watches Gabe

for a few seconds and then turns back to me with a worried look on her face.

"But maybe we should tell him about the vampires. I don't want him wandering around in a drunken stupor at closing time, and you know . . ."

I bite my lip. I've signed a confidentiality agreement with the town, but for the first time I'm getting to know some of the people I'm supposed to be protecting, and it seems beyond wrong to keep Gabe in the dark about what's going on. I look around the bar. There are at least a dozen people in here and I want to stand on a chair and yell a warning to them all. I sigh. I know I can't, but at the very least I can make sure Gabe survives the South Bristol vampire epidemic.

"We're not supposed to tell people, but what the hell? What's the use in being a slayer if you can't protect your man? There's no guarantee he'll believe us."

"We have to try. And I want to make sure he gets home okay. Um." She grimaces. "I know your mom is all big on racking up kills, but after our drink can we drive Gabe home? I could give you guys some money to make up for any losses."

"That's okay. I'll just tell her the Harkers were too efficient and after our first kill they kept beating us to the punch."

She exhales. "Thanks, I don't think I could concentrate on the vampires if I was worrying about Gabe." She opens another sugar packet. "And maybe one kill is enough for tonight—you know, I'm still learning the ropes and I don't want to push my luck."

"I think we should rename you Kiki Crusher, Reluctant Vampire Slayer."

Kiki looks down at the sugar packet in her hand. "Maybe."

Kiki frowns as we pull up to her cottage. "Maybe I should've invited him to stay over."

"Even though he thought we were making up the vampire stuff, I think he'll still be cautious. I'll bet he believes more than he was willing to admit."

"I hope so."

She elbows me. "Look who's here."

Tyler is leaning against one of the large stone statues by the front steps. Without waiting for Sam, we get out of the limo. "How many did you get?" Kiki asks.

"Ten total. You?"

"Just the one," I say, looking him in the eye and daring him to make fun of us. "We figured you had all the slaying taken care of so we directed our efforts into protecting citizens."

He cocks his head. "Isn't that what I was doing too?"

"We were protecting my boyfriend," Kiki says.

I look at her, surprised to hear her call Gabe her boyfriend instead of the usual "asshole." "Yes," I say. "We personally escorted him home. But add our total to my parents' eleven and we're ahead."

"Does this have to be a competition?" he asks wearily.

I shrug. "No, I guess not."

"Good," Kiki says. "Let's go in and relax. I think we should pop some champagne to celebrate my retirement."

My stomach drops. "What? Why?"

She takes my hand and leads me up the steps. "Slaying vampires sounds like a lot more fun than it actually is. I just don't think I have what it takes."

"Of course you do! Look at the way you totally got that vampire to come after us—that was genius."

Tyler scoffs.

"It was," I insist. "And what about how you staked that vampire on your first try? You're a natural."

"I've almost peed in my pants about a dozen times since I started this and my stomach has been in a perpetual knot. And look—I've broken out in hives." She points to the small red welts dotting her chest.

She looks back at Tyler and me. "I think this is something you have to be born doing." She sighs. "Besides, in a couple of days you'll be gone anyway," she says forlornly. "But you better promise me you will never ever hunt alone again!"

"Yeah, okay," I say quietly.

She opens the front door and starts spinning the prayer wheels.

"Stop!" Tyler says sharply.

Kiki jumps in surprise. "Oh, my God, what?"

He puts out a hand and stops the two wheels that are in motion. "You're spinning them backward."

Her shoulders relax and she laughs. "So?"

I look at the wheels trying to figure out how that could possibly be a problem.

"You're supposed to spin them clockwise—you know, like in the direction of the sun moving across the sky."

Kiki puts a hand on her hip. "And you know this because . . ."

"My dad has a prayer ring. He told me that if you spin it counterclockwise whatever you're praying for will manifest itself in a more 'wrathful' way. And with the weird energy lines here I'd be extremely cautious about what you're wishing for."

Kiki frowns at the wheels. "I've been wishing for the same thing since my parents had them installed, and trust me—it's not going to come true."

"What did you wish for?" I ask.

"That my parents would disband The Disco Unicorns."

Tyler's eyes pop. "Your parents are in The Disco Unicorns?"

"Lead singers."

"Wow. I didn't watch the show too much." He grimaces. "No offense, it was a little girly. But that's totally cool about your parents."

She rolls her eyes. "Not as cool as you might think, but I'll leave that sorry tale for another day. Come on and let's make a toast to my fabulous contributions to the world of vampire slaying."

We're sitting on the third floor lounging on pillows and surrounded by several empty champagne bottles. "I think she's asleep," I say, pointing to Kiki who's lying with her head back on a pillow.

"Yeah."

I giggle. "She's snoring."

He nods.

"I think I'm a little drunk. I've never had champagne before, but I kind of like it."

"Yeah, champagne was never in our budget."

"Oh, God, is your dad constantly going on and on about money like my mom?"

"It never ends. I can't tell you how many times we've had to sleep in the car. The thing that pisses me off is I was looking over his shoulder a few months ago at an ATM and we have *a lot* of money saved up. When I confronted him he just said you never know when the work will dry up and he's saving for a rainy day."

"I wish the work would dry up. If I never see another vampire again I could die happy. Don't you wish our parents were doing *anything* but this?"

He looks out toward the dark windows—the thinnest sliver of moon hangs just above the trees. "No. I'm good with it," he says quietly.

I crawl over to him on my hands and knees and look him in the face. "Come on, you can't seriously tell me you're okay with killing vampires."

"Yeah. I am."

I lean back onto my heels. "Are you crazy? I mean, I would give anything to just walk away from it all. I can't imagine why you wouldn't want to."

"Because they killed my mother."

I bring a hand to my mouth. "Oh, I'm sorry. I should have realized. I feel like a complete idiot."

"It's okay. I don't really remember her, but my dad is *always* talking about her—telling me stories, making sure I know what she was like. She would have been a great mom, I think. My dad has a lot of faults, but he made sure my mom wouldn't ever fade from my mind. And for every vampire I kill I know I've probably saved someone's life — maybe someone's mother. It's kind of like your mom. After her family was murdered, she —"

I sit up with my heart pounding. "What?"

In the dim candlelight I can see Tyler's eyes widen. "I — I thought you knew."

"No! What happened?"

"Oh, jeez. I think you should hear it from your parents."

"Tell me!"

He takes a deep breath. "Um, when she was sixteen her boyfriend got turned by a vampire. He showed up at her house and, without realizing what had happened to him, she invited him in."

"Oh, God."

"He killed her parents and her three younger sisters — ripped their throats out right in front of her," he says grimly. "He saved her for last because he wanted to turn her so they could be together. Our dads and your grandfather rescued her just as the guy had broken down the bathroom door she was hiding behind."

"*Sharon*. I've heard my mom mutter that name when we were house-cleaning. I wonder if that was one of her sisters?"

He nods. "Yeah, that was one of her sisters. My dad told me about her family. He talks about your mom and dad all the time, actually. It's kind of like he got stuck after what happened to my mom and lives in the past."

I feel sick to my stomach, as tears gather in my eyes. "Why didn't she tell me?"

"Come here," he says gently. He takes me in his arms and I sob into his chest. "It's okay," he whispers.

"It's not okay. I get so damn mad at her for being so cold and so crazed about this never-ending hunt we're on, and all this time she was living with this—keeping it locked up inside."

He strokes my hair.

"God, if only I had known."

"It's not your fault. They should've told you."

I pull away from him and wipe my eyes. "I'm sorry." I sniff. "Your shirt is all wet."

I wipe his chest with my shirt sleeve and he leans in until his face is inches from mine. His breath warms my cool lips and my entire body is on fire. "It's okay," he whispers.

"Are you, uh, sure?"

"Daphne, can I . . ."

I close my eyes and will myself not to faint. "Yes."

I wait for what seems an eternity with my heart pounding, and then gasp as I feel his hand brush some hair from my cheek. His fingers linger on my face leaving a trail of electricity. His lips touch mine gently at first, and then my mouth opens and oh my God he's kissing me.

I'm kissing *him.*

"Revenge," something cold whispers in the air.

We pull apart and look wildly around the room.

"Hunger."

Smoky black shapes are flying around just outside.

Kiki sits up groggily and puts her hands over her ears. "I'm having that dream again."

"Seek."

I stare out the windows with wide eyes. Dark shapes blacker than the night are flying across the river in a direct line to the house. Strange whispers fill the air making my skin crawl. Tyler reaches out and wraps me protectively in his arms.

"What the hell is going on?" Kiki wails.

"Kiki, get away from the window!" he commands.

She scrambles to his other side and he draws her close.

Dozens upon dozens of black shadows swoop around and then zip off into the night.

As they disperse, one shape hovers outside the glass in front of us. The creature appears to be made of undulating smoke. I can almost make out a woman's face and bare breast, and then bloodred eyes appear and lock onto mine.

The thing drags sharp claws along the window making goose bumps pop up on my arms. *"Revenge. Mother comes,"* it hisses before flapping batlike wings and flying off.

Soon the only sound is our labored breathing. I can feel Tyler's heart pound against me.

Kiki gulps. "What the fuck was that?"

I look up at Tyler. "What were they?"

"The lamia."

13.

Sam stops the limo at a light and Tyler squeezes my hand. I yawn and lean my head against his shoulder. Kiki's chin dips toward her chest a little and she gives a start.

"Did I fall asleep again?"

I nod. I'm thinking none of us slept very well. After what we saw, we hightailed it out of Kiki's house and Tyler brought us back to the motel. Luckily my parents didn't see us get out of his car. It was weird being with Mom after what Tyler told me though. I tried to change the way I look at her and the way I react to the things she says, but I couldn't help but get mad at her like always.

She smelled the champagne on my breath and accused

me of being drunk, completely dismissing what we saw. And she gave Kiki an earful about being a bad influence.

At least Dad got her to agree to let me spend the day with Kiki since it was likely we'd be moving on to our next job soon. Mom just wanted to do one more night, and then let the Harkers clean up the rest.

Of course we had to promise there would be no alcohol involved. At first I was surprised Tyler's father gave him the day off so he could come with us, but unlike Mom, Mr. Harker seems to be encouraging us to spend time together. Also unlike Mom, he thought it was a good idea to find out what we could about the lamia. Tyler had strict orders to meet his father downtown tonight no later than sunset.

I catch Kiki smiling at me. *So cute,* she mouths.

I roll my eyes, but can't help smiling back at her. I try not to think about leaving them both. I purse my lips and will the tears gathering in my eyes to go away and vow to enjoy every last second I have with them.

Kiki sits up. "Pull over there, Sam."

A small purple sign reading DARK SIDE EMPORIUM: PROPRIETOR RUPERT WOODS hangs over a dark stairwell leading down to a basement shop. Sam pulls the limo to the curb. He takes in the skulls and weird statues in the window, and turns to Kiki. "Picking up something for your parents?"

"Just doing a little research."

He shakes his head. "Will we be heading back to California soon, Ms. Crusher?"

From the tone of his voice it's obvious he's had enough of South Bristol.

Kiki slumps down in her seat. "Yeah, when Daphne leaves we'll head back. I'll be staying with her at the motel until then."

"Very good." He goes to open his door but Kiki puts a hand on his shoulder. "We got it, thanks."

As we walk into the Dark Side Emporium the first thing that hits me is the smell of some horrible incense. The small, narrow shop is filled with oddly shaped candles, bins filled with bones, black feathers, and dried herbs.

"This is creepy," I whisper and Tyler takes my hand into his. I look up at him and feel my eyes watering again. It's so not fair all this is going to be taken away from me so soon.

"Watch where you're walking!" a deep voice barks.

I jump and realize there is a very tiny man sitting behind the counter.

"Don't mess up my salt," he continues, waving a metal prosthetic hand at us.

Kiki points to the floor at the base of the counter and we all take a step back. Salt has been used to "draw" a circle around the counter.

The man looks at me with dark, sunken eyes. "You never know what might pop up and I need to keep myself protected. Demons and such can't cross the line."

We exchange looks and the man scoffs. "You kids don't know shit. What're you doing here anyway? You don't look like the type that should be shopping in here. Go home and play your video games."

"Mr. Wood, we need some information about the lamia," Kiki says.

The man's squinty eyes widen. "This got to do with what's happening in South Bristol?"

"Yes!" I say. "How did you know?"

He smiles, revealing a large gap between his front teeth. "Oh, we're all talking about what's happening to them kids. It's a shame, but nothing's to be done about it. Them's not ordinary demons—old as Adam and Eve they are. Made of smoke and fire so they can't be caught. Can't be trapped."

Tyler takes a step forward, clearly being careful not too get to close to the salt. "We think we saw them last night—we think we know the general vicinity they're coming from."

The man nods. "I've only seen drawings of them— right scary things. But something's opened a doorway to hell. That's what's attracting all the vampires."

"You know about the vampires, too?" Kiki says.

"I know a lot of things, and whenever there's an opening to hell the vampires come out of the woodwork—like they can hear their souls calling to them from the pits of hell. I'd take a vampire any day over what's coming though."

Kiki raises her eyebrows. "Something *else* is coming?"

"Those creatures sneaking out of the mouth of hell preying on infants are the children of the demon Lilith. I just heard they had the first fatalities so that means Lilith is close to showing herself. She is most powerful during the new moon, and once she arrives there's gonna be a lot more deaths and she'll fly farther and farther away from the opening each night, spreading carnage in her wake. And she don't just go after the children." He gives Tyler a look and clucks his tongue. "She likes to taste the blood of young men and pregnant women just the same."

"And I thought vampires were scary," Kiki deadpans.

I swallow the bile rising in my throat. "I know demons are supposed to be bad, but why would Lilith do that?"

"Revenge."

I shudder and can hear the awful voices in my head as if the lamia were in the room with us.

The little man hops off his stool and picks a large white crystal off the counter. "Come closer; one at a time—mind you don't cross the salt."

"I'll go first," Tyler says.

The man reaches over the line and I realize he's missing two fingers on his remaining hand. He waves the crystal up and down like a metal-detector wand. "You're good." He tilts his head toward me. "Now you, Red."

After Kiki and I both fail to elicit a response from the crystal the man steps over the line and walks to a bookshelf. "Can't be too careful. I've had demons come in looking like right ordinary people before. I don't trust anyone anymore."

He hobbles over to a bookshelf and scans the titles. "You there, big guy. How's about you get that book for me—the one with the red cover."

Tyler walks over and takes the book the man is pointing to and gives it to him. The man places it on a table crowded with bowls of different kinds of polished rocks and a bowl of what might be dried rat tails.

He flips through the pages, clucking his tongue and shaking his head until he turns to a page showing a drawing of the creatures we saw last night.

"That's them!" I say.

He smiles appreciatively at us. "You can count yourself lucky you had a sighting. Can't say there are many people who get a chance to gaze on a rare creature such as this."

"Lucky us," I mutter.

Mr. Woods clucks his tongue again. "There are varied stories about the origins of Lilith and the lamia, but she or something like her appears in Jewish, Greek, and Sumerian lore, just to name a few. Some accounts say she was the first wife of Adam who refused to lie beneath him and flew out of the Garden of Eden to cavort with demons, giving birth to hundred of the lamia each night. God sent three angels to bring Lilith back to the garden. When she refused, they threatened to kill her children and they did—a hundred a day. Lilith and her demon offspring fly out at night seeking revenge by taking the lives of innocents."

Kiki raises an eyebrow. "You seem to know an awful lot about this."

Mr. Woods shut his book. "I did a lot of research when I heard what was going on. I heard there was a big payout for whoever could help the town out. Unfortunately, the only way you can stop Lilith from rising from hell is to summon angels or a sympathetic demon. I don't know anyone who's summoned an angel and lived to tell the tale." He holds out his disfigured hands. "And with demons there is always a price."

"Angels are good though," I say. "Why wouldn't they want to help?"

Mr. Woods laughs. "Angels consider themselves far

superior to the likes of us, and don't like to be called like dogs to attend to human affairs. They're more likely to strike you down dead than to help you. Many demons, on the other hand, enjoy getting out of hell. The trick is not to let them get the upper hand. So to speak."

Tyler looks at Mr. Wood. "Do any of the stories offer suggestions about other ways Lilith can be stopped? Or ways to protect yourself from her?"

"Jewish lore says a charm or amulet engraved with the names of the three angels sent after Lilith can be worn around the neck and the sight of them repels her and the lamia."

"A charm with a couple of names on it can repel demons?" Kiki asks skeptically.

Mr. Woods looks at her with narrowed eyes. "There's a lot of power in a name. That's why demons go by so many, so you can't guess their real one and control them. But there are a lot of simple things that repel demons too." He points toward the counter. "Can't get any simpler than salt, and burning sage—they loathe that."

"Do you have any of those charms you mentioned?" I ask.

"I can make 'em for you. I do a lot of custom charm work. Takes a bit of time," he says, clanking his metal claw on the table for emphasis.

"We'll wait for them. One for each of us," Kiki says.

Mr. Woods eyes her. "You got three hundred dollars?"

"Yes," she replies.

He scrunches up his face. "Dang, I should've charged you more. But if you're willing to pay three hundred I'll get to work right away."

"Do you have any information about summoning angels and demons?" I ask.

"Look on the shelves—reading's free."

Kiki looks skeptically at me. "Do you really want to go there? I mean, look at what happened to him," she says in a hushed voice.

"It won't hurt to read about it. And who's to say he knows everything there is to know about angels?"

"We've got nothing better to do," Tyler says.

Kiki nods. "Let's hit the books."

An hour later we leave the store with our amulets dangling on silken cords tied around each of our necks. Mr. Woods engraved angel wings on the front and the names Sanvi, Sansanvi, and Semangelat on the backs. We're loaded up with a boxes of salt and incense that could be used to summon either a demon or angels, if we decide to go that route.

As Sam pulls away from the curb Kiki picks up the

incense and runs it under her nose. "Blech! If I were an angel I certainly wouldn't want to have to appear in the smoke from this stuff. I'd totally *smite* down anyone who tried it."

We'd read that if you were to evoke an angel that the "ethereal smoke" from incense was the substance in which they could be seen. The book used the word "smite" a lot, which had Tyler leaning toward trying for a demon. Mr. Woods recommended a few demons people had some success controlling that might be convinced to close the opening to hell—for a price.

"I think it would be really foolish to try for angels," Tyler says. "They're too powerful."

"But I'm partial to keeping my hands and fingers intact," Kiki says, waving jazz hands in Tyler's face.

"Yeah, I'm really leaning toward angels too. It seems counterintuitive to get some unreliable demon to do our bidding and not know if he'll take a limb in return."

Tyler looks at me. "That might be bad, but it could be worse. Have either of you ever seen the movie *Raiders of the Lost Ark*?"

Kiki nods. "Like, a gazillion times!" She fans her face. "Harrison Ford was so freaking hot! Why did he have to get old and wrinkly?"

"I've seen it too." I smile at Kiki. "And I agree with your assessment."

Tyler gives me a look.

"Don't worry," Kiki says. "Daphne thinks you're totally hot."

Tyler's red cheeks mirror mine.

He takes a deep breath. "Anyway, do you remember the end when they opened the ark and unleashed the power of heaven?"

Kiki's mouth drops open. "Oh, my God! All of their faces melted off."

Tyler nods.

"That was just a *movie*!" I insist.

Kike bites her lip. "I like my face, and I paid too much money to get my nose fixed only to have it melt off. Besides, Mr. Woods was pretty adamant about not summoning demons over angels."

"Are you forgetting he lost a hand and a half to one?" I shoot back.

Sam clears his throat. "My grandfather was a preacher and he warned his parishioners that if they ever desired divine intervention never to summon angels—"

"See!" Kiki says. *"Never summon angels!"*

"May I finish, Ms. Crusher?" he continues.

"Oh, sorry. Yeah."

"He told them to simply ask for God's help and if the Lord deemed the request worthy, He would send the necessary angel."

"Did your grandfather ever do it?" Kiki asks.

"Yes. If he's to be believed, angels led a school full of children trapped in a fire right through a flame-filled doorway."

I look at Tyler. "See? Angels!"

Kiki leans back in her seat. "I don't want to get smited, though."

"God and Lilith go back a long way. I'm thinking he's not going to want her running amok again."

"Okay, I guess I'm in. Angels it is," Tyler says.

Kiki nods. "Based on Sam's recommendation, I concur."

"Good," I say. "We're agreed. And really, I'll bet angels are way better than dealing with vampires."

Kiki grimaces. "Now we just have to figure out where the opening to hell is. Let's just hope we come out with our faces still on when we do."

14.

We pull up to Kiki's cottage around four o'clock and she gasps. "My parents are here! Sam, did you know they were coming?"

He looks at Kiki in at the rearview mirror. "It's just your mother. She called me to see how you were doing. You might want to take her calls once in a while, by the way. But I may have expressed some concerns. She was planning on coming out anyway. Apparently she has some news for you."

Kiki leans over the seat and swats him gently on the shoulder. "Damn it, Sam, this is like the worst time ever! You should've told her not to come!"

We get out of the car and the front door opens. Kiki's

mother stands in the doorway with her arms spread wide. "Maybelle! Darling, let me look at you."

Kiki groans. "Mom, don't call me that!"

"She's *Maybelle*?" Tyler whispers to me.

"I thought you didn't watch the show."

"Okay, I did kind of sometimes watch it." He turns to me—eyes wide. "If you tell anyone, I can't be responsible for my actions though."

Mrs. Crusher sweeps down the stairs with her long brown hair flowing around her waist instead of done up in the usual sleek Disco Unicorn "mane" she sports on TV. "Sam told me you had some new playmates."

She smiles at Tyler and me while Kiki scowls.

"I'm not three, *Mother*; these are my *friends*, Daphne Van Helsing and Tyler Harker."

Mrs. Crusher puts her hands together as if in prayer and bows. "I'm so happy to meet you. *Namaste*."

Tyler and I copy her and bow in return. "Nam-as-ty," I answer back, butchering the word. I hope I haven't said anything highly offensive in whatever language she was using.

Mrs. Crusher puts an arm around Kiki. "As much as I'd love to have your little playmates stay and meditate with us we have some very important business to discuss."

Kiki gives me a look. "Business. Right. I'm fine by the way."

She pats Kiki on the top of her head. "Of course you are, darling. Perhaps your friends can meet up with you after I leave."

"You're not even staying the night?"

"Alas, no. I have a five a.m. interview with *Good Morning, Portland* and I need to meet with our press secretary to find the best way to do damage control now that Sugar Leblanc is with child."

Kiki's mouth drops open. "Sugar got knocked up?" She laughs. "Wow."

"Maybelle!" she snaps. "This is no laughing matter. We just launched a new line of Sugar action figures that we won't be able to give away now."

"What does this have to do with me?" Kiki asks.

"Darling, we want you back on the show! We had focus groups look at your photos while listening to your recordings and you got a favorable rating with ninety-one percent of our respondents when you were billed as Princess Peony, the Lost Unicorn Princess. Our focus group is wild about your new look, and we can announce to our fans that our beloved daughter is joining us onstage for the first time in twelve years. The press will eat it up, and Sugar's indiscretion will be relegated to a one-inch blurb at the back of the tabloids."

"Unbelievable," Kiki says.

Mrs. Crusher beams. "I know! It will be so nice to have you back on the Pink Pony Playhouse stage. But let's head inside so we can discuss the details." She turns to Tyler and me. "So very nice to meet you, and don't forget—think only pinkish wonderful thoughts!"

Kiki glares at her mother. *"Mom!"*

"I'd be happy to give you both a ride home," Sam says. "Thanks."

Tyler holds the door open for me and I marvel how my world has been completely knocked out of its orbit in the last few days. The saddest part is, when we leave South Bristol, it'll be right back to where it was—as if Kiki and Tyler had never existed.

Dad pulls the van up to The Rusty Rudder. "You sure you want to do this?"

"I don't have anything else to do—might as well see if I can score a few more for Team Van Helsing." And call Kiki and Tyler and tell them I'm leaving early. Hopefully they can come down so I can see them before I have to go.

"Team Van Helsing?" Mom asks.

"It's nothing. Just something Kiki made up."

"Okay, then," Dad says. "We'll finish getting our things together, pick you up, and then it's off to Providence. You probably don't remember much of the city, Doodlebug.

You were pretty little last time we were there, but we took you for a camel ride at the zoo."

"Wow. Sounds awesome," I deadpan.

"Watch the attitude, missy," Mom says. "Maybe you can actually make a few decent kills now that the Crusher girl isn't around to hold you back. She was a gamble that definitely did not pay off. This whole job was a nightmare from start to finish."

"But we're not finishing it—we're running away."

"*Enough,*" Mom snaps.

I squeeze my eyes shut and bite my tongue to hold back a string of expletives. "I *really* think we should stay and look into the lamia. If we could stop them we'd be saving a lot more innocent lives"—I turn to Mom—"and make *a lot* of money."

"We heard everything you had to say about it, and we made our decision," she says. "We're not going to deal with angels or demons, Daphne. We'll leave that to the Harkers."

"But Mr. Woods said they'll be most powerful on the night of the new moon. Look." I point up to the sky. "No moon. And two babies have already died. Do you want more deaths on your conscience?"

Mom stiffens. "What do you mean by that?" she asks tersely.

My heart races. "I didn't mean what happened to your family," I blurt out.

She whips around to face me. "*Damn Harkers*. They told you, didn't they?"

"Tyler thought I already knew. But it wasn't your fault, and that's not what I meant before. I was just talking about the babies and how we should try to help before the lamia get any more of them." I bite my lip. "But why didn't you tell me?"

Mom looks to Dad. "It's not something I like to think about."

"But you do—you think about it all of the time. I can tell."

"Daphne, let it go," Dad warns.

"We need to talk about it. It changed your whole life and I think if you just admit there was nothing you could've done maybe you could finally realize you're not responsible for saving the world—"

"Honey, stop," Dad says.

"But this is my life too, and because she's been carrying around all this guilt I've had to get dragged around the country killing freaking vampires! What kind of life is that?"

Mom bows her head. Her shoulders start to shake and for the first time in my life I see her crying.

"And I don't think you should blame Mr. Harker for his wife getting turned. No one forced her to join that Ankh Society. That poor man is carrying around as much pain as you are—maybe more. Give him a break."

I wait for either one of them to respond. When they don't, I open the door. "Call me when you're ready to leave on our next adventure."

I get out of the van and slam the door shut. I look up and down the street, hoping to spot Tyler, but there's just a middle-aged woman walking a small dog that yaps at me as they approach. "Be careful, there are vampires prowling around," I tell her as she passes me.

She scoffs and hurries her dog along—repeatedly looking back over her shoulder at me. "I'm not kidding!" I add.

She takes out a rattling set of keys, unlocks a door and with one last look, slips inside. When I see a light flicker on in an apartment above the florist shop, I head into the pub.

It's a Saturday night and there are a lot more people here tonight. So much for Dad's theory. I scan the room and my stomach drops. Tyler is sitting in a booth with a girl who has draped herself all over him. She's giggling and whispering in his ear—he's laughing in return. She pulls her fingers through his long hair and I'm about to run out when he catches my eye for a second. Like an idiot, I wave, only to see him push some hair from her face, his hand lingering on her cheek.

Oh, my God. My last night here and Tyler is working the vampires. Touching her face the same way he touched mine.

I turn and stalk out of the pub. I head for the alleyway leading to the back and pray there'll be a vampire I can slam a stake into!

I'm such an idiot. I actually imagined that Kiki and I were going to keep hunting vampires together and Tyler and I . . .

"God, this sucks!" I scream. "Why does everything in my life always have to be so freaking disappointing?"

"Daphne?"

I jump and turn. "Gabe." I put my hand over my heart. "You scared me." He's leaning against the building with a cigarette dangling from his fingers. "What are you doing back here?"

He hangs his head. "Same as you. Getting away from it all. Having a smoke. Is Kiki with you?"

"No," I say as my heart slows. "Her mom flew out to talk to her. They want her back on the show. For all I know she's on a plane heading for L.A. right now."

"She won't do it."

"How do you know?"

"Because I know Kiki—she wants to be on Broadway. She wants to be the next Kristin Chenoweth. "

"Who is that?"

"A really amazing Broadway star—been in a few movies too. She's Kiki's idol. I've heard Kiki sing. I think she could make it."

I walk over and lean against the wall next to him. "She never mentioned that to me, but I hope she blows The Disco Unicorns off and moves to New York City if that will make her happy."

"Or she could stay in South Bristol with me."

"Yeah, that would be cool except for the vampire problem. I know you think we were bullshitting you last night, but it's true. South Bristol is fucking loaded with stupid vampires."

"I know."

I nod. "I had a feeling you believed us."

"I didn't—not until my friend showed up."

"Friend?"

"Remember I said I was looking for my friend, Michael?"

"Oh, no . . ."

"I'm afraid so."

He taps his cigarette and over an inch of ash falls to

the ground. "I'm so sorry, Gabe." I reach out and grab his hand—it's icy cold.

"No." I try pull away but Gabe squeezes my hand so hard I gasp. I look at him and see a red glow in his darkening eyes.

Gabe licks his lips. "I'm sorry too 'cause right now *I'm starving.*"

In a flash he throws his cigarette down and puts a hand on my throat, pinning me to the wall. He leans in and sniffs my skin. "This is going to be so good. I can already taste you."

He pulls back revealing sharp fangs.

"Please, Gabe. Let me go." I kick out at him, but he clutches my throat tighter and I struggle to catch a breath.

He drags his teeth across the nape of my neck and a moan escapes my throat. "Just relax."

I nod. My mind is fogging over and the only thing I can feel are the tips of his teeth teasing my skin.

"You want it, don't you?" He pulls open my shirt exposing more of my chest. He traces the scratches with his cold fingers and plants his icy lips on the puncture wounds. "You've been tasted before." He licks the wound and my knees buckle.

He hoists me up in his arms. "Tell me you want it."

My head is screaming to yell for help but all I can do is keep nodding.

"I was hoping it'd be Kiki tonight, but I can't wait any longer, and you smell so freaking good." He plunges his teeth into the base of my neck and I inhale sharply. With every suck from his mouth my troubles fade. I just want it all to go away.

"Get off her!"

Gabe's mouth is ripped from my neck and I collapse onto the ground. Tyler punches him in the face and is on him like a wild cat when he hits the ground. In an instant he plunges a stake in Gabe's heart and then takes a knife out of his trench coat and beheads him in two swift strokes.

Gabe's face is frozen in a look of shock. I turn away and throw myself at Tyler.

"You're okay now," he says, taking me in his arms

I shake my head as tears stream down my face. "No, I'm not. I'm never going to be okay. I'm so tired of this and Gabe is *dead*! How am I going to tell Kiki?" I suck in a ragged breath.

"I'll go with you."

"We're leaving tonight."

"I won't let you go," he whispers, kissing my hair.

"Please don't say that just to make me feel better," I sob.

He grabs me by the shoulders and looks me in the

eye. "We'll figure out a way to be together. I promise you. Here . . ." He takes a bandanna from a pocket in his trench coat and presses it against my neck.

He leans into me and my mouth finds his. My hands rake through his hair as I urge him to kiss me harder.

He pulls away. "I have to tell you about before—she's a vampire. I was just trying to get her to come outside so I could—"

"It's okay. I know."

"I'm *so sorry* I hurt you."

"Just hold me," I plead, needing to feel grounded to someone, even if it's just for short time.

"Daphne, what are you doing?"

I lift my head up from his chest. Mom and Dad are standing side by side with grim expressions on their ashen faces. "What does it look like, Mom?"

"Joy, let it be," Dad warns. "He's going to need all the support we can give right now."

"What's going on?"

"Tyler," he starts. "We got a note from your father; he slipped it under our motel room door."

Tyler's eyes widen. "What does it say?"

"He's going after the lamia," Mom says. "But he isn't planning on returning."

Tyler looks back and forth between my parents. "What?"

"He asked us to take care of you—and if anything happens, we will," Dad says. He looks at Mom and she nods solemnly.

"Dad, what do you mean he's not planning on coming back?"

"The note was kind of rambling, but he's been tracking those ley lines for a number of years, hoping to find some sort of nexus point that was powerful enough to provide an opening to hell."

"Oh, my God," Tyler says. "He's always said he wished there was a way to go to hell and rescue my mom's soul. He's always spinning his prayer ring—always wishing."

"And Kiki, too," I say. "You said she was spinning the prayer wheels backward—encouraging a wrathful wish fulfillment. Maybe they both were, and now their wishes have come true in a twisted mess. There's an opening to hell for your father, and if the lamias aren't stopped, there won't be any kids for Kiki's parents to entertain."

No one says anything.

"Daphne," Mom says finally. "Where did you see the lamia?"

"They seemed to be coming from directly across the river from Kiki's house. There are a lot of large boulders on the other side. Maybe there's a cave or something."

Dad takes the van keys out of his pocket. "Let's hurry."

15.

We pull up to Kiki's and she races out of the door and down the steps. "What are we doing?" she asks breathlessly. "Still angels?"

I look at my parents and Tyler. "Angels?"

Everyone nods even though we all look unsure. We're definitely treading in unfamiliar territory.

"Okay," Kiki says. "I've got my sunglasses, we can head down to the dock."

I hold my hands out. "Sunglasses? It's nearly midnight."

She nods. "Yeah, you know—in case of heavenly face-melting rays. Does anyone else want a pair?"

I cock an eyebrow. "Do you really think sunglasses will keep your face from melting off?"

She shakes her head. "Yeah, forget it. If we melt, we melt. I've been spinning the prayer wheels ever since you called, though." She looks at Tyler. "Clockwise."

"All right, then," I say. "Flashlights on. Let's head down to the water."

"What time did the creatures come out when you saw them?" Dad asks as Kiki leads the way to the dock.

"Around this time—midnight."

"We better hurry," Mom says.

We rush to the dock and carefully pile into Kiki's boat where Sam is waiting for us.

"Nice to meet you," Dad says to him.

"You can meet me just fine after you find your friend. Everyone hold on."

"You are so getting a raise!" Kiki says.

"Damn right I am," he agrees. He starts the outboard motor and a chill runs through me as the boat speeds out over the water.

"Look!" Tyler says. He points to a faint light up on the cliff side. "That's got to be where he is."

I reach out and squeeze his hand. "We'll get him," I call out over the sound of the wind and the motor.

"Oh, my God," Kiki squeals. "They're coming."

Dark shapes are flying out from the rocks near the light. They swoop down and fly past us, filling the air with their unholy whispers. I shudder. If Lilith can give birth to a hundred a day, who knows how many there are.

"Hunger."

"New moon," one says as it passes by my ear.

I flinch and cover my mouth and nose, to avoid breathing in the sulfuric stench left in its wake. Mom ducks her head and Dad puts an arm around her.

"These aren't the ones you need to worry about!" I call out. "They're just after the babies to get revenge for their mother."

I hold my charm out and the lamia dash away screaming like they've been dowsed with holy water. Kiki and Tyler see what I'm doing and hold theirs out too, making the creatures scatter on the wind, giving the boat a wide berth.

We bump along in the choppy water and I hope we're not too late. I squeeze the charm around my neck tightly in my fist and visualize the name of the angels on the back. "Help us so Lilith can't return and we can bring Mr. Harker home safely," I repeat, over and over again until Sam slows the boat at the opposite shore.

"There's no place to dock here!" Sam yells. "You'll have to jump to shore—be careful 'cause that water's freezing."

We all nod. He puts one foot on the rocky beach and tries to keep the boat steady as he helps us out. The stench on the shore is overpowering and the air is thick with whispers and maniacal laughter.

"Hurry!" Tyler calls out.

We start scrambling up the rock face—trying to keep our balance while shining the light for possible hand and footholds. Warm air pours down from above carrying the lamia as they joyride out across the water.

"Are we almost there?" Kiki calls out.

I look up—a small point of light glimmers just five feet above. "Yes! Keep going."

Tyler reaches the ledge first and helps pull us up. The heat and smell are almost unbearable and I imagine it will be far worse in the cave.

The creatures screech and cackle as they fly by. I hold out my charm, relishing their anguished cries as they dodge to avoid it.

"Maybe you should stay out here," Dad yells out.

"No!" I say. "We're all here—we all have to believe."

"Let me go first," Dad says. As he enters the cave, the exiting lamia weave around him—some circling a couple of times as if to see if he might be something of interest.

Mom and Tyler follow him, but Kiki pulls on my arm before I go in. "I'm scared," she whispers. "Really, really scared." She looks up at the dark sky. "Once again, in theory this sounded like a good idea and I pictured myself being really brave, but the reality—not so much."

I take her hand. "You don't have to do this," I repeat, though I know she will.

She nods. "Oh, I'm going to—I'm just not going to like it. But if we don't make it out of this, I wanted you to know I'm so glad you found me. Even though I didn't make the greatest vampire slayer, these have been the best, and the *freakiest*, three days of my life."

A tear runs down her cheek and my eyes water up. "I couldn't ask for a better BFF."

She holds out her arms and we embrace. Part of me thinks I should tell her about Gabe, but I decide that can wait. No sense putting her through any more anguish than need be in what could be our final moments.

"We better go," I say, pulling away. I hold out my fist and she bumps it with hers. "Let's hope the angels aren't in the mood to smite anyone but Lilith tonight."

We slide sideways through the narrow opening. The passageway widens to a small chamber with a high ceiling. The lamia are clawing their way out of a four-foot wide, fire-licked fissure that bisects the hollow. Once free, they spread their wings and rise to the top like smoke coming out of a chimney stack. They circle and claw at each other in midair before swooping down and exiting the chamber, no doubt to head out for victims.

In the flickering light, I can see the lamia are not as smoky and hastily formed as they were when they appeared at Kiki's—perhaps the power of the new moon has allowed them to fully manifest themselves. Here they appear as red-eyed, bare-breasted monstrosities with women's heads and torsos atop black snakelike bodies with tattered wings propelling them through the night.

Kiki puts a hand on my arm. "Look, on the other side—Mr. Harker."

"Nathan!" Dad yells out.

We all turn, but I'm finding it hard to see with all the creatures moving about in the flames. I can just make out Mr. Harker sitting cross-legged in the middle of a pentagram enclosed in a circle. White candles burn in the tips of the star, and from what I can tell, it looks like it's made from salt like the one Mr. Woods had in his shop. He's rocking back and forth spinning his ring, and muttering to himself. I'm not sure how Mr. Harker was able to get the other side of the fissure—unless he got there before it opened to the fiery depths below—but it's clear we can't get to him.

"Dad!" Tyler calls out. *"Dad!"*

"Nathan!" my father yells.

Mr. Harker either can't hear, or he's choosing to ignore us.

Tyler turns to me with tears in his eyes. "How are we going to get across?"

I look helplessly at him. "We can't jump through the flames." If Mr. Harker wanted to get into hell I'm wondering what he's waiting for—but maybe the fire is keeping him from going in, like it's keeping him from us.

"*Nathan!*" Mom screams. "*Nathan! Damn it, look up!* Vince, he can't hear us! It looks like he's in some sort of trance."

"What should we do?" Tyler implores.

"Kiki, get the incense out!" I yell.

She puts her messenger bag on the ground and I help her take out seven large cone-shaped incense candles. We line them up on the stone floor, and, using a grill lighter, she ignites the tips of each one. Thick, fragrant smoke pours from each one and the lamia in the cave fly to the entrance as if driven out by the smell.

My heart pounding, I press my amulet to my chest. "*Help us.*"

Dad and Mom join hands and bow their heads. I turn and see Kiki slowly putting on a pair of sunglasses. She looks at me and shrugs. Despite everything going on I can't help but roll my eyes.

Suddenly, the lamia still clamoring to get out of the fissure start shrieking and fly out as if the devil himself was on their tail. My ears ring as they screech *"Lilith"* and *"mother"* louder and louder. A delicate hand grasps the top of the fissure and a beautiful woman pulls her way out.

I'm mesmerized by the sight of Lilith rising into the chamber propelled by her reptilian body. Long, shiny, dark curls glisten in the firelight and fall perfectly over her pale, bare chest. Her face is almost angelic, but her snakelike bottom half is scratched and scarred as if she'd fought a long battle to get here. Large, glossy wings unfold and flap—fanning the flames—making them lick and scorch the top of the chamber. She breathes deeply and stretches her arms over her head, then tilts her head back and screams.

Mr. Harker jerks up—panic clear in his eyes. "No! It's not ready!" he cries, looking up at the creature. "The fire is still burning! Why is the fire still burning?"

Lilith undulates across the floor toward him, weaving like a cobra.

"No, stay back!" he says. He looks past her at the crack in the floor. "No!" he howls. "You're supposed to leave and the fire is supposed to die and then I can find Rebecca."

"Dad!" Tyler calls out. *"Dad!"*

Lilith winds her body around the salt circle he drew. She tries to cross it, but howls in pain as smoke rises from her scales. She then turns to us, and her red eyes bore into mine. I try to catch my breath, but I find myself gasping in the putrid air.

Kiki shrieks and she grabs my arms *"Daphne, don't look at her!"*

My mouth opens but I can't take a breath. Lilith licks her lips with a forked, flickering tongue and opens her mouth revealing sharp teeth. I find myself walking toward the flames—wanting to be with her—when suddenly I'm hit from the side.

"Daphne!" Mom cries. She yanks the necklace off my neck and holds it toward Lilith. "Stay away!"

Whatever spell Lilith had me under is broken, and the creature turns from the charm Mom is brandishing.

Mr. Harker's eyes widen in horror as he finally realizes we're in the cave too.

"Tyler, what are you doing here? Get out while you can! All of you! Now!"

"I'm not leaving without you!" he calls to his father.

In a panic, Mr. Harker gets down on all fours and frantically wipes the salt across the floor, destroying the protective circle.

"Nathan, no!" Dad screams.

His protection gone, Lilith is on him in a flash. She drapes her sinewy arms around him like a lover would and Mr. Harker's eyes seem to glaze over. She speaks to him in a language I don't recognize, as the tip of her tail wraps around his waist and lifts him up. Without warning she draws back her lips and lunges at his neck tearing at his flesh.

We all scream in horror.

"We need to get out of here!" Mom calls out. "It's too late for Nathan."

"We can't leave him to die!" I protest.

"Look!" Kiki cries out. "In the smoke."

I turn and see a face forming in the smoke pouring up from the incense. As the smoke curls and twists, snatches of bodies and wings and swords appear. A second face is joined by a third. Whenever I'd imagined angels, I pictured calm and serene presences, but these faces are brutal and harsh and I have to look away.

"Lilith!" voices booms, echoing around the cave.

The commanding sound vibrates through me and almost takes my breath away.

Lilith turns and howls at the angels. She throws Mr. Harker down like a rag doll and slithers toward the crevice. Blood drips from her mouth and stains her snow-white chest. My legs are shaking so badly it's difficult to keep upright and I clutch Tyler's arm.

She continues to rant in some ancient tongue and I wait for the angels to strike her down. Lilith seems to sense their inaction and gives an evil smile that would scare even the deadliest snake. She slides back to Mr. Harker and picks him up as if he were as light as a feather.

"No!" he chokes out, as her tail wraps around his waist. "I have to find Rebecca!"

"Oh, my God!" Tyler screams out, as his father beats Lilith's chest with his fists to no avail.

She teases her fingers through his hair and then grabs a handful, pulling his head to the side, letting her tongue flick in and out as she laps up the blood.

I turn to the smoky faces shifting in the smoke. *"Please help us!"* I beg. *"Please!"*

Suddenly, the smoke whips away and forms a tornado-like cloud in the middle of the chamber, drawing the flames up higher and higher. Strange sounds and chanting ring in my ears as the wind gets stronger. Faces of the angels growling and screaming appear fragmented in the dust and smoke and flames swirling over the fissure.

Then I hear the river as loud and choppy as if we were still on the boat. A hurricane-force wind whips into the cave and I'm ripped from Tyler's arms and thrown to the floor. I frantically claw at the ground and water is forced into my mouth as I'm pulled toward the opening of the crack.

Even though we're halfway up the cliff, water is flooding the cave as if a dam had just broken loose. Dozens of the lamia wash in and bump against me—their waterlogged red eyes stare up blankly as they're tossed in the current and swept into the fissure that is now sending up billows of steam. Others are being pulled into the cave and they claw helplessly in the air as the wind drives them toward the mouth of hell.

Suddenly I realize Mr. Woods was right about angels. They can help, but not always the way we want them to. We've summoned them to help us—and they are—they're pulling the lamia back into hell, but it's apparent they won't stop *us* from going in as well.

"They're flooding the cave!" I call out—spitting water out of my mouth. "If we don't get out of here we'll drown or get sucked into hell!"

Lilith drops Mr. Harker and flies to the ceiling, screeching like a banshee.

Mom and Dad are heading my way with Tyler, and I grab Mom's hand and they help her pull me up as the water gets higher, fighting its pull toward the fissure.

Kiki screams as she's knocked over and swept toward the crack in the floor. We form a chain and rush after her.

I grab the back of her hoodie, and we all pull to help her scramble back up.

Across the fissure Mr. Harker slowly pushes to his knees. Most of the water is heading down the crack so the ground on his side is relatively dry. He puts a hand on his neck and surveys the chamber. "This is what I was waiting for."

"*Dad!*" Tyler cries as he clings to whatever handholds he can find on the wall. "I'll come and get you."

"No!" Mr. Harker insists. "I have to do this. I've been waiting sixteen years for this. Take care of him, Vince."

Mr. Harker crawls on his hands and knees toward the fissure. He looks up at Tyler with tears in his eyes. "I love you and I hope you can forgive me someday." He scoots over to the edge, and without another word, lowers himself into the abyss.

As if the earth had been holding its breath until this moment passed—it roars to life and the walls begin to shake. Large pieces of rock splash into the growing tide. Lilith flaps her wings and dives down as if to escape through the passageway, but every time she does a gust of wind rushes in to chase her back, slamming her into walls. She claws at the rocks for purchase and screeches angrily as her wings tatter from the beatings. Strange voices roar above the howl of the wind, and flashes of swords and faces surround her in the smoke and steam.

Her frustrated screams pierce the air, and she finally dives toward the fissure carried by a hurricane-force gust that follows her back into hell.

I see Tyler's eyes riveted to the spot his father disappeared down. *"Tyler, come on!"* I scream. The water is pouring in up to my knees, and the wind gusting into the cave is making it harder and harder to stay upright.

Tyler takes one last look, and moves just before the wall he was leaning on crumbles and washes away.

He pulls himself along the wall against the rising water, and I can see his fingers bleeding as he scrapes them against the rock to make his way to us. By the time we reach the opening my hands are bleeding as well, as I fight to keep from getting swept away.

Dad reaches out and pulls me toward the entrance. The water is up to our waists. I see now that it's pouring up from the river like a waterfall in reverse. There's no way we can climb down.

"We have to jump."

It's mid-April in Maine and I wonder how long it will take for hypothermia to set in.

The earth trembles again and we put our hands out to shield ourselves from the falling rocks.

"Daphne!" Dad yells. "Jump! Mom and I will follow you."

My lip trembles. "I love you all." Tyler fights to get to me and takes my hand and I reach back and pull Kiki toward the edge.

We squeeze hands and jump into the windswept air.

16.

I stick the end of a pencil under the edge of my arm cast and pray I can reach the itch.

Kiki laughs at me. It's good to hear her laughing again, even if it is at my expense.

"The itching is driving me crazy. I can't believe I have to wear this for two months."

"At least this forces you take a vacation from slaying."

Tyler walks in from her kitchen with a plate of nachos and puts them on the coffee table in front of me. He sits on the couch and gives me a half smile. I'll take it. Since his father voluntarily entered the mouth of hell just a week ago, this is the best he's managed. I slide my free hand into his and lean in and kiss his cheek. He leans his head onto mine and I hope he can forget, even if it's just for a second.

I follow his gaze and look out the window across the river at the decimated cliff. The newspapers are still buzzing about the localized "earthquake." We're lucky we survived, and if Sam hadn't fished us all out of the water, we probably wouldn't be sitting here.

"So you're going to do most of the talking, right, Kiki?"

"Yeah. How do you think they'll take the news?"

"Hopefully they'll take it a little better than your parents did when you refused to go back to the Pony Playhouse. But it doesn't matter. There isn't anything they can do about it."

We eat until the doorbell rings. My stomach flutters nervously as my confidence wanes.

Kiki opens the door and leads Mom and Dad in. They look around with puzzled expressions and Mom puts her hands on her hips. "Where are your things? I told you we'd be here at four—plenty of time to get in your last good-byes."

I take a deep breath. "Tyler and I aren't going with you."

Mom raises an eyebrow. "Excuse me?"

Kiki clears her throat and straightens her spine. "They're coming to New York City with me. I've already rented a place overlooking Central Park for Daphne and me to share. Tyler is going to room with an ex–Disco Unicorn dancer who works on Broadway."

Mom straightens her jaw. "Not funny, girls."

"We're not joking," I say.

"Doodlebug, you're only seventeen," Dad says.

I fold my arms across my chest and will myself to feel as confident as Kiki looks. "I'll be eighteen in two months, and Kiki's lawyers are drawing up the papers so I can file to become an emancipated minor."

"This is ridiculous!" Mom snaps. "Now get your things and get going — you too, Tyler."

Tyler sits up and puts an arm around my shoulders. "We have interviews with the NYPD vampire task force set up for next week. Officer MacCready has already sent in reference letters for us — and he told us they need new people, so it looks good that we'll get hired."

Mom scoffs. "I don't care if you have an interview with Santa Claus with glowing references from the Easter Bunny; you are both coming with us!"

"Dad?" He looks at me and I plead with my eyes. "You know this is better for me. You two are suited for traveling around — I've never stopped wanting to settle down. It's time I get to live my own life."

Mom scoffs. "You're not old enough to know what you want. And after the near-constant complaining you've done about hunting vampires, I find it hard to believe you'd actually want to interview for a job doing just that."

I look up at Mom. "I want to keep fighting, but I want to do it on my terms. I want to do it for your sister, Sharon—for your whole family." I hang my head. "And for Mrs. Harker and Gabe."

Kiki sits next to me and squeezes my hand. "Sam and his boyfriend will be living on the same floor as us. So we won't be totally on our own," she says.

"And Mom, you were basically on your own at an early age. You were sixteen when you decided to go with Dad and the Harkers. Maybe you need to keep moving around because it makes it easier to forget your home, but that's all I've ever wanted. I need to stay in one place. I want a home for myself; maybe even take some college classes—plan a backup career."

Mom looks at Dad. "I don't know. . . ."

"Joy," Dad says. "She's been slaying vampires since she was twelve—more often than not, alone. I think she needs to spend time with people her own age. What if we all go together, see them get settled in. And we can visit as often as you want to make sure things are okay." He turns to me. "Can you handle your old man seeing you off—coming for visits at the drop of a hat?"

I rush up and hug him tightly. "I would like nothing

better." I pull away and look at Mom. "Please understand."

Mom chews on her bottom lip. "Daphne . . ."

"I need to do this—just like you need to . . ."

Her eyes soften and glisten with tears. "Okay, we'll
give it a try. But I guarantee you'll be calling us to pick
you up within a month."

"Maybe," I say, but we both know it isn't true.

Kiki squeals and shakes her fist. "We're going to
NYC, baby!"

New York City
June

I stare at my reflection in the elevator doors as Kiki and I head up to our apartment. "I still can't believe you found the dress."

Kiki somehow located the light purple dress I had in my binder for my fantasy prom date. "I felt a little silly wearing it home though."

Kiki waves a hand dismissively in the air. "Liar! I saw you loving the stares you were getting."

I smile and point a foot out in front of me to admire the jeweled high heels she bought too. "Maybe a little. I'll pay you back for the shoes when I get my first paycheck. Now that the cast is off they finally put me on the schedule. With Tyler, of course."

"Hey, it's my treat—all of it. Happy birthday."

"Well, I'm a little overdressed for the restaurant we made reservations for, but what the hell. I just hope Tyler won't feel funny—I told him it was casual."

She looks me up and down. "I don't think he'll mind."

"Well, you need to get dressed up too, so I won't feel out of place."

The elevator doors open and we walk down the hall to our apartment. She rifles through her purse and then looks at me. "I think I left my keys on the counter—can you get the door?"

"Sure." I fish out my keys and unlock the door. Tea lights are draped around the house plants and hanging from the ceiling. A cardboard pineapple tree stands next to a small table covered in a pink paper table cloth. A punch bowl sits on another table with bowls of chips and dips.

"What is this?"

She beams at me. *"It's prom."*

"What?"

"P-R-O-M. Prom!" She runs to the counter and docks her iPod. Music blares out of the speaker and she quickly turns it down a bit. "Hmm. *There's something missing,"* she says loudly.

On cue Tyler walks out of my bedroom looking slightly embarrassed in a dark gray tuxedo. A purple rose is pinned to his lapel and in his hand he has a corsage made up of more purple roses mixed with baby's breath.

"Wow. You look . . . *stunning*," he says quietly.

Tears prick my eyes.

"What's the matter?" he says nervously. He looks at Kiki. "Did I say something wrong?"

I throw my arms around him and bury my face in his neck. "You said everything right!" I pull away. "You guys are the best."

Tears stream down my cheeks.

"It was actually Tyler's idea. I was telling him about how you were always moaning about missing the prom. The setup is all me, though. Oh, and there's one more surprise."

"I don't need anything else—this is perfect."

She smiles smugly. "Just wait." She runs out of the apartment and I hear her knocking on Sam's door. Suddenly the hall erupts with barks.

I shake my head. "No."

I turn to Tyler who's laughing. "Yes."

Kiki leads in with a small white dog on a leash. "It's not a puppy, but I thought with our schedules we'd be better off with an older dog that doesn't have to go out every two hours."

I kneel down and the dog rushes over to me and sniffs

my hand. I reach out and melt as I stroke his incredibly soft fur.

"I don't know what to say."

Kiki picks the dog up. "Say hello to Fang."

I run my fingers down his silky ears. "Hello, Fang." I lean in and let him lick my chin and cheeks.

Kiki puts him on the floor and heads toward the door. "Since I don't have a date, I feel kind of funny going to the prom. I'm going to take Fang to Jerry's apartment so we can run lines."

"Are you ready for opening night?" Tyler asks.

"Yup! Thank goodness I got the boobs done—I was made for this part. Well, with a little help from Dr. Marx. But *A Chorus Line* has never seen a better Val. I sing the crap out of the Tits and Ass song, if I do say so myself. But I'll leave you two alone." She looks at me. "Don't do anything I wouldn't do."

She leads Fang out and I turn to Tyler. He holds out the corsage. "May I?"

I shake my head and take it from him and put it on the table. "There's something I want to do first." I take his hand and lead him to my room. I point to the bed. "Sit."

He grins, his eyes locked onto mine.

I reach behind and slowly unzip my dress, and let it slide down my shoulders.

His mouth opens a little as he takes a jagged breath. I watch his eyes roam my body as I carefully step out of the dress pooled around my feet.

My pulse quickens as I walk slowly toward him. He stands up and wriggles out of his jacket and tosses it aside. I reach out and start to undo his bow tie, leaning my chest into his. I pull off the tie and throw it on top of his jacket. I tilt my chin and gently bite his lower lip as I unbutton his shirt. He's breathing hard as I slide the shirt down and off his arms and then put my hands on his bare chest. I look up at his face and stare into his eyes.

"You have the most gorgeous eyes," I say.

"I love you," he whispers as his hands slide down my waist.

I can feel his heart pounding and I push him down on the bed. "I love you, too."

"Aren't you going to take your shoes off?"

I turn the light off. "Nope!" I slide onto the bed next to him and we wrap ourselves around each other.

"Happy birthday, babe," he whispers.

As his hands move around my body I almost laugh. Tyler Harker is my boob guy after all.

Interview with Kiki Crusher for *Jennifer-Kate* Magazine

JK: You're a former child star and you've recently made your Broadway debut in the most recent revival of *A Chorus Line*. What prompted you to open a huge can of worms and petition for *Gabe's Law*?"

Kiki: I lost someone near and dear to me to a vampire attack, and realized it was time for the world to finally be informed about what is out there. Nine out of ten people will never meet a vampire, but if people were given even the basic information about them, my boyfriend, Gabe, might still be here. There are other paranormal creatures people should watch out for too—why not let the American public be forewarned and prepared?

JK: Aren't you worried about the backlash? Congress has said outing vampires will change how people go out at night, crippling the economy.

Kiki: Knowledge brings power. With the newly released information, people are getting the facts about how they can protect themselves—and getting the garlic spray I've helped patent. The public has everything they need to ward off any potential attacks. I have friends in the slaying industry and they've noticed a tremendous decrease in fatalities. Gabe's Law is helping save lives. And my show has been sold out every night—not bad for a revival!

JK: What about all the bogus "remedies" and "protection sprays" popping up?

Kiki: Only buy ones with the FDA approval seal on them.

JK: Obviously you disagree with The Ankh Society's claim that vampires are harmless, but they really believe people and vampires can coexist. What would you say to them?

Kiki: Vampires kill. The Ankh Society would like us to believe getting bitten by a vampire is a harmless way for the creatures to feed without killing and for its members to have some fun—but the bottom line is, a creature without a soul can't be trusted. And the bite is as addictive as heroin. I know someone who lost his mother to just such a scenario. Vampires and humans are never going to be a good combination.

JK: Well, I know there has been a tremendous amount of support—and controversy—about outing vampires. But that's what we at *Jennifer-Kate* like to applaud. Do you have a few more minutes to take our *Quick-Five Question Challenge*?

Kiki: I'd love to!

JK: Chocolate or coffee?

Kiki: Coffee! I strive to be in a perpetual state of caffeination.

JK: Last book you read?

Kiki: *The Encyclopedia of Demons and Demonology.* A must-read for everybody!

JK: Favorite designer?

Kiki: Christian Siriano. I'm a sucker for reality TV.

JK: Celebrity crush?

Kiki: Sutton Foster. It's my dream to star on Broadway with her.

JK: Favorite charity?

Kiki: Proms for Everyone. My cochair, Daphne Van Helsing, and I make sure prom dresses and tickets are available to everyone who wants to go.

JK: Thanks for talking with us. Be sure to catch Kiki in the revival of *A Chorus Line* now playing on Broadway and keep an eye out for her forthcoming autobiography, *Playhouse of Broken Dreams*.

Here's a sneak peek
at another novel by Amanda Marrone

DEVOURED

Nicki rounds the corner fast, and I clutch the arm rest tightly. I take a deep breath and see her look my way.

"Oh God, sorry," she says as she takes her foot off the gas pedal and presses on the brake. "I get carried away on this stretch."

I look out at the river hugging the road and will myself to take in the gorgeous White Mountains scenery instead of imagining the car skidding off into the water. "Hey, no problem," I lie. "And thanks for driving me. Figures my mom has one of her stupid dog things the day I get the interview. She and Fergus have a new routine, and this is the first time they're performing it."

Nicki laughs. "How could she retire the 'Toxic' number? That was a showstopper!"

"Ha, ha, funny."

Of course my mom dancing with our golden retriever in front of an audience, and then posting the videos on the Internet is anything but funny. "Anyway, I swear I'll do *all* the driving when I get my license."

"Don't worry about it, Megan."

"Seriously! I'm gonna do it this time. I signed up for lessons with this new driving school that just opened."

Nicki pushes her long bangs out of her eyes. "I believe you."

I know she's really thinking I'll chicken out like always, but I'm grateful she doesn't say it out loud. She knows that despite the years of therapy, riding in a car still freaks me out.

She takes the turn onto Enchanted Boulevard like a ninety-two-year-old grandmother would, and I point to an office building near the entrance to the park. "The interview is over there."

She pulls into the nearly empty parking lot, which will be jam-packed in a week. "Are you sure you really want to do this?" she asks.

I stare up at the Land of Enchantment sign. Smiling princesses and overly cute forest animals wave their animatronic arms. Even as a kid I wasn't crazy about coming here all that much — the crowds, the two-minute rides that never seemed worth the long wait to get on them. But Remy loved everything about Land of Enchantment, and Dad used to say he'd never seen a pair of twins look at the world so differently.

A small shudder wracks my body. It's been ten years since Remy died, and ten long years of being haunted by her ghost. Coming here is just asking for her to pop up, and I'm wondering if I can pull off an interview with Remy's ghost babbling in the background. I'm very tempted to tell Nicki to put the car in reverse and go home.

But I don't.

"I was getting sick of the bookstore," I lie. "Ever since Diane got promoted to manager, she's been a total bitch. And this way I'll be outside getting a tan instead of spending another summer paler than a vampire."

Nicki shakes her head. "This has nothing to do with getting a tan and you know it. I've kept my mouth shut so far, but to be honest, getting a job here because you're afraid to leave Ryan and Samantha alone is kind of stalkery."

"*Stalkery?* Since when did wanting to spend time with your boyfriend become stalking?"

Nicki gives me an incredulous look.

"Okay! The thought of him and Samantha working together has been driving me nuts, but can you blame me?

She's been his best friend since second grade, and we've only been going out for three weeks and two days."

"This is so not like you! Where's the Megan who'd never chase a guy she just started seeing? Who'd never in a million years *stay* with said guy if she didn't trust him?"

I stare up at the prince on the sign, climbing Rapunzel's long braid. "*That* Megan was tired of not having had a relationship since freshman year. And *that* Megan was confident things were strictly platonic between them until Samantha made one too many trips to the keg and made her 'soul mate' confession. Not to mention the fact that she's totally gorgeous—and nice. How can I compete with that?"

"Yeah, that was *real* nice of her to make a play for Ryan while you were in the bathroom. But despite her drunken confession, he's still with you, so what are you worried about?"

I shrug my shoulders. "I don't know. I just wish he hadn't told me about it."

"He was being honest with you, and if you ask me, that's a good sign."

"Or maybe he was laying the groundwork for our breakup—so it won't come as a big shock when he tells me he's finally realized the girl of his dreams was living right next door all along."

Nicki shakes her head and takes out her iPod. "Good

luck. Hope they assign you to something cool like the hot dog cart. Or if you make a really great impression, maybe they'll give you one of those little brooms and dustpans with the long handles, and you can sweep trash from the walkways."

"Actually it's always been a dream of mine to work the slushy machine, but what I'm really looking forward to is spending the summer endlessly repeating 'Welcome to the Gingerbread Coaster, please keep your hands inside the car until the ride comes to a complete stop.'"

Nicki puts the earbuds in. "I'm gonna listen to some songs; the tryouts are tomorrow and I still haven't decided what to sing." She turns the volume up and I can hear "Defying Gravity" from *Wicked*. "Working at any of the fast-food joints on the outlet strip would be better than this," she says loudly.

I pick up my purse and tell myself I'm above spying on my boyfriend. But then I think about how being with Ryan makes me feel more alive than I have in years, and I open the door and head for the park offices.

I sit in front of Mr. Roy and put on the best I-would-so-be-an-asset-to-your-amusement-park smile I can muster. Looking at his Cinderella tie, I have a feeling he'll be a pushover.

"So . . ." He glances down at my application. "*Megan,* why do you want to work at Land of Enchantment?"

Telling him I've turned into a stalker because good-girl Samantha morphed into a man-stealing bitch is probably not the best approach, so I straighten up, look into his washed-out gray eyes, and lie. "I've loved the Land of Enchantment since I was a little girl, and nothing would make me happier than the opportunity to put a little magic into some kid's summer vacation."

I smile harder and hope I didn't lay it on too thick.

Mr. Roy tilts his head and beams. He clasps his hands under his chin. "Is there a special memory of the park you could share with me? I always love hearing how we've affected people; it's what keeps me going when the day-to-day operation details get overwhelming."

Oh, God, what to pick? Toddler throwing up on the teacup ride? Third-degree sunburns from standing in endless lines? Eating warm egg-salad sandwiches because my parents were too cheap to buy lunch at the park?

"Um, well, I remember this one time, I think I was maybe five, and I was scared to go into Hansel and Gretel's Haunted Forest, and then someone tapped my shoulder. I turned around and there was, uh . . ." My mind scrambles to come up with something plausible. "Uh, there was Snow White. She held out her white-gloved hand and said, 'Don't worry, sweetie; I'll go in with you.' With Snow White by my side, I knew I could do it, and to this day Hansel and Gretel's Haunted Forest is one of my favorite attractions."

Mr. Roy looks teary, and it's all I can do to keep from rolling my eyes. Hansel and Gretel's had to be the lamest thing here—half the animatronics were broken, and the scariest thing about it was that the fact anyone actually paid money to see it.

"Well, Megan, I think we have a spot on our enchanted team for a special girl like you. I see you've checked off ride operations, gift shop, and character actor on your application. I'd bet a bundle you were hoping to fill Snow White's gloves yourself, am I right?" He leans toward me and winks.

Don't roll eyes! "Yes, sir, 'Snow White' is one of my favorite stories, and it would be so much fun to play her."

"What a coincidence. 'Snow White' is one of my favorite stories, too. And with your dark hair, you'll be perfect! Unfortunately, you can't be Snow White every day; we try to mix up our team member's experiences so everyone gets a better feel for the park, and we can find those special kids who turn their Land of Enchantment summer jobs into a life-long career. After all, you'd never know whether you have the makings of our future Fun

Farm manager if you don't get to spend some time in the Billy Goats Gruff pen—which we go to great lengths to keep clean."

I smile like this is a wonderful opportunity, all the while praying to God I won't be shoveling crap all summer.

"Your next step is to meet our team coordinator—my wife, Miss Patty."

He winks at me, and I will myself to keep the wide-eyed smiley expression plastered on my face.

"She'll give you our orientation packet and training schedule, and get your size for the costume."

He picks up his phone and pushes a button. "Honey bear, I'm sending a new recruit down." He glances at my application again. "Megan Sones. You'll need to take her to the costume room for a Snow White fitting." He pauses and smiles at me. "She's perfect." He hangs up and pushes his chair away from his desk. "Patty's office is just around the corner. I'll point you in the right direction."

I look around at Miss Patty and her office and I'm thinking she has some unresolved issues that a few years of therapy *might* make a dent in. The walls of her office are bright pink and adorned with portraits of princesses with oversize lightbulb-shaped heads rendered in Day-

Glo pastels. PATTY is signed in huge six-inch letters in the bottom right corner of each one, and I wonder how she could've willingly signed her name to these atrocities. Completely out of place with the rest of the décor, a ratty stuffed boar head hangs gathering dust above an overly gilded mirror just behind her desk.

"Megan," Miss Patty says with a hint of a Southern drawl as she extends a well-manicured hand with rings on each finger. "It is such a *pleasure* to meet you! I'm Miss Patty, your enchanted team leader, and it's my job to get you ready for your enchanted summer!"

"Nice to meet you," I say, trying not to stare. High, pointed arcs have been drawn on her forehead way above where her eyebrows should've been, and one of her false eyelashes is crooked. Her face has a brown leathery look to it—like she's spent way too much time in tanning booths—and her curly blond hair extensions don't match the rest of her overly processed, thinning hair.

Miss Patty points to a pink polka-dotted chair and I sit. I look up at the boar's yellowed tusks and ratty fur and can't understand why this woman, who's obviously very concerned with her appearance and the color pink, would have something so totally gross in her office.

"Here's our introduction packet. It has the W-2's and emergency contact forms you'll need to fill out, plus general park information, shift times, and a training schedule. Do you know CPR?"

I nod, picturing myself performing CPR in the Snow White costume, and wonder if it's too late to run screaming from her office.

"Excellent!" She opens a folder and scribbles something on the paper inside. She looks up at me and flutters her thick eyelashes. "Oh, I would kill for a complexion like yours!"

I hear the door behind me open and turn to see a girl about my age with a thick white-blond ponytail and ice blue eyes. "Patty, Daddy said you had some things for me to file," she says.

Miss Patty frowns. "Ari, can't you see I'm with a new team member?"

Ari stares blankly at her. "I just need the paperwork and I'll be out of your way."

Miss Patty smiles again, but her eyes bulge slightly as if it's taking a great deal of effort to do so. "Megan, this is my daughter, Arianna."

"Hey," Ari says, and she gives me a look like she knows her mom is in serious need of some counseling and/or medication.

"Articulate as ever," Miss Patty mutters.

Ari rolls her eyes and I almost wish I were back with Mr. Roy.

"Nice to meet you," I say, trying to act like there isn't an incredible amount of tension smoldering in the air between Ari and Miss Patty.

"I'm not quite finished with the paperwork, Ari," Miss Patty says. "You'll have to do it tomorrow."

"But I've got auditions tomorrow."

Miss Patty lets out a long sigh. "Auditions are not all day long. Surely you'll find some spare time."

The phone rings, and Miss Patty holds up a finger to me. "Just a second, Megan, honey." She fluffs her hair with her hands, like whoever is on the other end might see her, and then picks up the receiver.

"Yes?" She takes a deep breath as her cheeks redden. "They were supposed to be here a week ago! How are we supposed to serve popcorn without bags? Look, hang on." She pushes a button on the phone. "Ari," she says sweetly. "Would you mind showing Megan where the costume room is and get her dress and shoe size on the Snow White clipboard?"

"Anything to help you out, *Patty*," Ari answers in the same syrupy tone.

Miss Patty picks up the phone again, and Ari tilts her head toward the door.

I take my information packet and follow her out.

"She's my *step*mother," Ari says as soon as she closes

the door. "She always forgets to add that part. She thinks just because she married my dad when I was like three that makes her my real mom." Ari gives me a sly smile. "It drove her crazy when I started calling her Patty a couple of years ago."

"I'll bet," I say, thinking that if I had a stepmom like that, I might like to stick it to her once in a while too.

"Anyway, she's a complete nut job—her new thing is shaving off her eyebrows so she can pencil them in. She thinks it makes her look like Pamela Anderson."

Knowing how it feels to have a mother who's slightly off, I decide to sacrifice my reputation in hopes of making her feel better. "Well *my* mom dances in competitions with my golden retriever."

Ari's eyes grow wide. "*Seriously?* She dances with your dog?"

"Yup! A fully choreographed, costumed routine. Google 'Fergus and Sally's Fantasy Freestyle' and you can see them in action for yourself. She's recently added footage of their new number, 'Hopelessly Devoted to You,' in which she's wearing a miniskirt she decorated with a BeDazzler."

Ari shakes her head in disbelief. "Wow! I guess both our moms are nutters, then."

I don't say anything and wonder if my mom was always

"nutters" or if it happened after the accident. No. I remember when she and I were close—when she'd let me help her cook. I was Mom's little angel, but now—now I'm nothing.

We walk down the hall, and I look at the old black-and-white photos of the park hanging on the walls. I'm actually impressed they were able to turn what looks like a glorified petting zoo and carousel into the halfway decent amusement park it is today.

Ari turns to me. "So you signed up for Snow White, huh? The bodice is itchy."

"You've been Snow White?"

Ari scoffs. "Patty makes me help out, but I draw the line at walking around the park in character. I've heard some of the girls complain about the costume, though. And here's a tip: If you're posing for a photo op with a family, try to keep the kids between you and the dad. Some of them are horn dogs who'll try to cop a feel while the flash is going off."

"Thanks for the warning," I say, thinking I should beg Diane to give me my job at the bookstore back.

We turn the corner and I gasp. Remy is standing at the end of the hallway, twirling one of her braids in her left hand. She waves. "Meggy," she calls out and starts walking toward us.

I turn to Ari, but she's rattling on about something to

do with her stepmother and Botox, oblivious to the fact that my dead twin is heading our way.

I just knew she was going to show up here! Go away, Remy!

"I said this is it."

Ari is pointing to a door labeled YE OLDE COSTUME SHOPPE. "Oh. Sorry, I, uh, was just thinking about what you said about the dads."

"Don't worry too much about it. The really bad ones tend to gravitate toward the Bo Peep girls. Something about the petticoat—or maybe it's the way they hold the staff that gets their shorts all aflutter."

I smile, but I'm really thinking I need to get out of here. I look past Ari, see the hallway is empty, and exhale. Hopefully Remy just appeared because she likes that I'm at the park, and not because she has something she wants me to see.

Ari opens the door and turns on the light. There are hundreds of brightly colored costumes hanging on rolling stands. "So," Ari says, looking me up and down. "Size six?"

"Eight," I say, wondering if she was just being nice. "And I'm eight in shoes too."

Ari heads to the Snow White rack and pulls out a costume. "Here it is, your golden ticket to playing friend of forest creatures and tiny little men!"

I groan. "Is it too late to cross 'character actor' off my application?"

Ari laughs. "Despite the potential for being groped, wearing a costume is actually a hell of a lot better than being chained to a ride for hours on end. Except for some scheduled stops in the park, you can pretty much do whatever you want. And you're lucky your hair is black. You won't have to wear the wig, which I'd bet sucks when it's ninety degrees out." Ari hangs the costume back up. "Can you sing?"

"God, no! Do I have to?"

"No, but Patty's been talking about maybe having a character sing-along."

"Yeah, I think my voice would clear the park, but my best friend sings. She's in the White Mountain Chorus. Actually, she's waiting for me, so I should—"

Ari's mouth drops open. "I'm in the chorus too! Well, I was last year, and I'm trying out again tomorrow. Who's your friend?"

"Nicki Summers, and like I said, she's waiting—"

Ari claps her hands. "Oh my God, I know Nicki! She has an *amazing* voice; she kept beating me out for solos. I can't even believe they're making her try out. I mean, everyone knows she's gonna make it. So she's here?"

"Yeah, she's in the parking lot, but Nicki told me the

old director left, so everyone's starting from scratch this year."

"Huh, I didn't know Mr. Sherman left. Of course he would've told Nicki—they were tight." Ari starts stalking around the costume rack. "I'd love to find out what she's singing. Let me put your info on the clipboard, and then I'll go out with you." She shakes her head. "Damn, it's not here. *Patty* probably left it in the laundry room. Let me run down and see if I can find it. Hold on."

As soon as Ari leaves, the temperature in the room rapidly drops. "Remy," I say, my breath frosting in the air. "I don't want to play with you." The lights flicker and a cold sweat breaks out on my forehead.

"Meeeeggy." Her voice echoes in my head. "I have something to show you."

I back up toward the door, legs trembling, and scan the room for Remy. "I don't *like* the things you show me, Remy."

The door slams shut behind me and I jump. "Fine! What is it?" I yell, sounding braver than I feel. I learned long ago that trying to ignore Remy just pisses her off, and I should get this over with before she starts throwing things.

Remy appears by the Snow White rack. Water drips to the floor from the hem of her dress and the tips of her braids. She frowns and beckons to me with her small seven-year-old hand. "Meggy, come see."

"What? The costumes?" I picture trying on clothes from the dress-up box Grammy gave us when we were five, and a tear rolls down my cheek. "I'm gonna play dress-up this summer, Remy—as Snow White." I point to the costumes and hope I can divert her attention from whatever it is she wants to show me. "Do you wanna see me put one on?"

Remy nods and puts the end of one of her braids in her mouth, and I remember how Mom used to dip the tips in Tabasco sauce, trying to break her of the habit.

I walk slowly toward her, and she points to a costume in the middle of the rack.

As I reach out for the satin sleeve, Remy touches my arm. An icy chill runs through me, and the room disappears. I see a girl wearing a Snow White costume lying on the ground in a wooded area. It's dark, and I squint at the black stain on her bodice. I bend down and realize the bodice is unlaced, and while the blouse is soaked in what I think is blood, the darkest stain is actually a hole—a hole in her chest cavity where her heart should've been.

"Be careful, Meggy," Remy whispers as everything goes black.

About the Author

AMANDA MARRONE is the author of *Uninvited*, *Revealers*, *Devoured*, and *Slayed* for teens, and the Magic Repair Shop series for younger readers. She grew up on Long Island, where she spent her time reading, drawing, watching insects, and suffering from an overactive imagination. She earned a BA in education at SUNY Cortland and taught fifth and sixth grades in New Hampshire. She now lives in Connecticut with her husband, Joe, and their two kids. You can read more about Amanda Marrone's work at www.amandamarrone.com.

The Cursed Ones have made their presence known,
and the world will never be safe again....

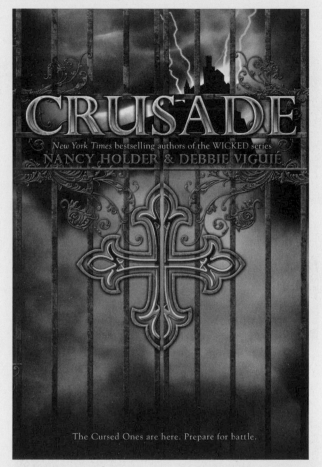

From the *New York Times* bestselling authors of the Wicked series
NANCY HOLDER AND DEBBIE VIGUIÉ

From Simon Pulse

Published by Simon and Schuster

From the NEW YORK TIMES *bestselling author of* THIRST NO. 1
REMEMBER ME
Christopher Pike

Her death will not go unpunished. . . .

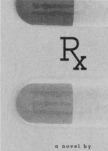
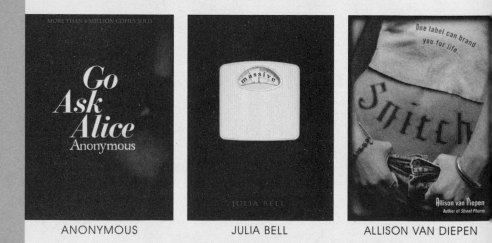

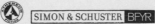

simonTeen

Simon & Schuster's **Simon Teen**
e-newsletter delivers current updates on
the hottest titles, exciting sweepstakes, and
exclusive content from your favorite authors.

Visit **TEEN.SimonandSchuster.com** to
sign up, post your thoughts, and find out what
every avid reader is talking about!